PRAISE FO

CW01501792

"Wren St Claire's ᵛ
Elisa Braden and Elizabeth Hoyt to mind. Her stories are so rich and she has a great way of making
the reader root for morally grey characters." Reader's comment

Masterful, moody and magnificent! 💙

Reviewed in the United Kingdom on November 4, 2023
<u>**Verified Purchase**</u>

⭐ ⭐ ⭐ ⭐ ⭐

Beautifully written, passionate and totally captivating. Haven't read a historical romance for ages
but loved this - now onto book 2! HIGHLY REC-
OMMENDED. 💋💙❤️😚💚

ABOUT THIS BOOK

Two governments are after him, domestic and foreign...

It was a hell of a time to fall in love...

Dr Merlow Thornton has come to Pinner to hide from the men who are after him. It couldn't be a worse time to fall in love, but one look at the Vicar's daughter, Miss Hetty Rooke and he's done for. If only he can convince Miss Rooke to trust him. But the adorable lass is determined to keep him at arms-length, and with danger on his tail, can he, in good conscience, pursue the woman he wants more than his next breath?

The man of her dreams...

Dr Thornton is everything, twenty-eight-year-old, Hetty has dreamed of, but behind her façade of perfect vicar's daughter lies a past scarred by shame. If the past will only stay buried, she might have a chance at happiness at last…

An old-fashioned courtship…fraught with danger and passion

While Merlow works to win Hetty's trust and heart, the dangers of village life draw them together, as their respective secrets threaten to tear them apart.

The Scottish Doctor is the heart-warming first book in The White Lotus, Steamy Regency Romance series. If you like swoony Scotsmen and small-town romance with a twist, then you'll love Wren St Claire's new series that mixes laughter, tears and gentle seduction with a touch of martial arts action.

The Scottish Doctor is a spin off from **Saving Mr Rooke, Book 3.5 of the Villain's Redemption Series**, in which both Hetty and the Doctor make an appearance.

The White Lotus Series: Where Scottish and Chinese cultures clash, with some unexpected results…

Series reading Order:
Book 1: The Scottish Doctor: Merlow and Hetty
Book 2: The Scottish Laird: Col and Aihan
Book 3: The Scottish Lass: Isa and Caishen

CONTENT WARNINGS

This book contains references to sexual assult, infant death and adult death, on page suicide and attempted suicide.

THE SCOTTISH DOCTOR

STEAMY REGENCY ROMANCE

THE WHITE LOTUS
BOOK ONE

WREN ST CLAIRE

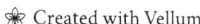

This one is for my late husband, twelve months on without you I have written seven and half books and as of this date, published five of them. Thank you for believing in me when I didn't believe in myself. I hope I've made you proud my darling.
Joseph Brian Campbell 26.5.1950 - 17.7.2023

THE SCOTTISH DOCTOR

Wren St Claire

PROLOGUE

Shangqui, Henshen Province, China, September 1813

"Sāng dùn!" insistent hands shook him awake. Merlow Thornton sat up with a start, blinking in the poor light from a single lantern.

"What?" he asked and then realising he had spoken in English, he repeated in Chinese, "What is it? What has happened?"

"Everything is at an end!" his servant, Lai Qui, knelt by Merlow's mattress on the floor of the room that had been his for the best part of ten years and wailed. "Master Zhanghu-Zi is captured and surely dead, the Rebellion has failed. We must flee, Sāng dùn!"

Merlow shook his head to clear it. He had feared this outcome. What possessed his Master, a man usually both level-headed and calm, to participate in a conflict so obviously doomed to failure, he would never understand. *But the man would not be talked out of it, and now this!*

"Hurry! We must hurry!" urged Lai Qui rising

to his feet and seizing a satchel and stuffing a package of food, a flask and clothes into it. "The Qing soldiers are approaching the village! They were passed on the road by the courier who brought the news. They are charged with killing all who profess to support the faith of the White Lotus and the Rebellion. If they see your tattoo, they will kill you!" Qui pointed to the red Baguadao tattoo on his upper arm, symbol of the White Lotus.

Merlow scrambled to his feet, finally galvanised into action, his heart thudding hard, his stomach roiling. His time here was done, whether he wanted it to be or not. Ten years of his life ended so abruptly...yet he had feared this outcome. He swallowed the lump in his throat and shook his head to clear it. No time for sentimentality in this moment.

He gathered up all his tinctures and as many ingredients and instruments as he could fit into another satchel, along with the texts he had gathered and notes he had made during his apprenticeship with Zhanghu-Zi, as well as his purse and some personal effects he brought with him from home. He hastily donned his Chinese style tunic and trousers, pulled on his boots, tying his long hair back with a ribbon and throwing a cloak over the whole.

He took the satchel Qui gave him. "What of you?" he asked, the young man who had served him for the last eight years. Fortunately, his strangely accented Chinese was understandable to his servant. A thick Scottish brogue had made it difficult to master the language, but persistence had paid off, and he'd managed to make himself understood.

"I will flee to my family in the mountains. I can lose myself there."

Merlow nodded. "Good, be safe my friend, and thank you for your years of service to me. I wish I had more to give you."

Qui shook his head, wiping tears off his face. "Master Zhanghu-Zi, left me a small purse in case of this eventuality. Come, I will saddle your horse," he said heading towards the stables.

"I'll meet you there in a moment," said Merlow grabbing a second lantern. Following him out the door and veering off towards the small square temple that stood in the centre of the rear garden he hurried up the steps and into the dim interior. He skirted the altar and went to a niche in the rear wall, where a hidden catch revealed a cache with two objects inside. The words of his Master reverberated in his head.

"If all is lost you must take the text and the sword and flee. If you return to your homeland the text will be preserved. There are few, if any copies left. You must preserve it for the future of humanity. Promise me you will do it Sāng dùn."

He had promised. So here he was, taking the text and the sword and fleeing as instructed. Binding the text to his chest beneath his tunic with a wide silk sash, he carried the sword in its scabbard. He made one last obeisance to the altar upon which rested the remains of the ritual performed only hours earlier, and made his way to the stables. Where he found Qui had saddled his horse. He attached the satchels and the sword to the saddle with straps, and turned to Qui.

"Farewell and may the Great Spirit keep you safe," he said, giving the young man a hug.

"And you Sāng dùn!" Qui sniffed and Merlow swallowed the lump in his throat, blinking back his own tears. He was returning home after ten years away, it was a wrench to leave this place where he had found himself, found his soul and his purpose. Would returning home prove a spiritual wasteland as he feared, or would he find a way to bridge the man he had been when he left, with the man he was now?

If he survived the journey of course...

London, June 1815

The Hon. Mr Durand Percival shifted uncomfortably in the chair waiting for the Prime Minister to get to the point. He was a good-looking man in his early thirties, with blond hair and blue eyes, a fine physique of which he was justifiably proud and the kind of confidence and affability that cut a swathe through the female population, but also made him well liked among men.

"Mr Percival, the British Government thanks you for your service." Lord Liverpool smiled apologetically.

Durand Percival uncrossed his legs and leaned forward, "I feel there is a but coming?"

"We rather hope we can persuade you to undertake another task for us?"

"What sort of task, my Lord?"

"You'll be aware of Amherst's upcoming Embassy to China?"

"Good heaven's you don't want me to go to China, do you?"

"No, no, my dear chap." He opened a file on his desk. "There's a Scottish fellow, has the most outlandish name... Ah here it is! Doctor Merlow Thornton. Second son of some Scottish Laird, hails from Fife. Fellow studied at Edinburgh and Paris and got a job as Chief Physician with the East India Company, spent some time on voyages to India and the East Indies before he joined George Staunton on a trip to China in 05. Do you know who Staunton is?"

Durand shook his head, which dislodged a blonde hank of hair he was forced to push off his face with a well-manicured hand.

"Staunton was the child prodigy that accompanied his father on McCartney's mission to China in '92. His command of the Chinese language was so proficient he was able to act as translator and even undertake banter with the Chinese. He was considered a crucial part of the success of the mission. He was twelve at the time."

"Impressive," remarked Durand, wondering what all this had to do with the Scottish fellow and whatever it was Liverpool wanted him to do.

"Thornton was, by all accounts, so shocked by the impact of the opium trade on the local Chinese he resigned his post with the East India Company and elected to stay in China. We lost track of him for years. He returned to Scotland last year, where we believe he still is, at his brother's home in the small town of Dysart, County Fife."

Liverpool shut the file and clasped his hands on top of it. "We want him for Amherst's Embassy. Staunton's going and speaks highly of him, believes he would be an asset, particularly given his medical training and years of living in China. He must be proficient in the language and have an excellent understanding of the culture by now.

"Your job is to recruit him for us."

Durand's shoulders relaxed. "Should be simple enough, I'd be happy to. The usual fee, plus expenses?"

Liverpool smiled and held out his hand. "Excellent, thank you, Mr Percival, we would be most grateful. There is some urgency to this matter. The Embassy party is scheduled to leave in January 1816, less than six months away."

CHAPTER 1

*M*iss Henrietta Rooke, Hetty to her family, eyed the big black bull between her and her destination, the O'Donnell's fence. *Drat! What was Old Fred doing down here anyway? He was supposed to be safely penned in his paddock up the hill.* Instead, here he was in the lower paddock blocking the shortcut to the O'Donnell's', whose property ran alongside Mr Beatson's, the proud owner of prize-winning Fred.

The problem was, her mind preoccupied with the list of tasks she had to accomplish that morning, she hadn't noticed Fred until she had climbed the stile and dropped down into his paddock. Now several steps in, she wasn't sure what to do. Hefting the basket full of goodies for the numerous O'Donnell children, she considered her chances of out running Old Fred or beating a hasty retreat to the fence line behind her.

"That's no a guid idea lassie," said a voice quietly behind her.

Doctor Thornton! Her heart skipped a beat at that lovely Scottish burr.

She glanced back over her shoulder at the man, who was leaning on the fence watching her with a broad grin through his neatly trimmed beard. His grey eyes twinkled in amusement. *The man was too damned handsome for his or rather her own good. How dare he laugh at her predicament.*

"What do you suggest I do?" she hissed exasperated.

"I'll distract the wee besom for ye," he said vaulting the fence as he spoke and waving to attract the bull's attention. *Gracious the man was mad. Fred might be old, but he wasn't decrepit, and he had nasty horns!*

"Oi laddie, over here!"

Fred, confronted with two intruders in his paddock, swayed his head between them, seemingly confused.

"Run lassie!" urged the doctor waving more vigorously at Fred. When she just stood there gaping at him, he moved and scooped her up into his arms, basket and all and ran for the fence line.

Looking over his shoulder, her nostrils full of the clean scent of soap and something spicy and exotic, she saw Fred lumbering after them. Clutching the basket and the doctors broad, tweel-covered shoulders, she suppressed a squeal of fright and hung on for dear life as Fred gained on them, his wicked horns lowering.

The doctor reached the fence line and dumped her on the top of the stile. She scrambled over, followed rapidly by Thornton as a disgruntled Fred reached the fence and swayed his head back and forth, snorting dissatisfaction at having missed his quarry.

The doctor bent over to catch his breath and laughed.

She straightened her bonnet and did her best to look offended. "I'm sure I don't know what you're laughing at!"

"Ye should a seen yer face lassie!" he said gasping and chuckling between breaths. He straightened and his grey eyes sparkled with mirth. But the laughter was kind and begged her to share in the joke. She choked and giggled and both of them leaned on the fence and had a good laugh, much to Fred's disgust.

When she could talk without giggling, she said, "What are you doing here?"

"Visitin' the O'Donnell's same as ye, but I was intendin' to take the road like a sensible person, instead o' riskin' life and limb crossin' a field with a bull in it!"

"Fred isn't normally in this paddock, and I didn't notice him until I was well inside the fence."

"How could ye no' see a bluidy great beasty like that?"

"I was thinking of something else," she said with dignity.

He smiled and shook his head. "Clearly ye shouldna be allowed out on yer own Miss Rooke!"

Her colour still heightened from the experience of being chased across a paddock by a bull and held securely in the arms of a strong, handsome man, smelling pleasantly of sandalwood and pine, she looked down at her skirt to inspect any possible damage, at a momentary loss for words. The good doctor had discombobulated her from the moment they met; a month's acquaintance hadn't lessened the effect. If anything, it had intensified.

"You're full of nonsense doctor!" she said making a recover.

"Am I?" he said taking her arm and helping her to negotiate a tussock of grass in their way.

She glanced at him, and her heart rate, which had settled after the mad dash across the paddock, unaccountably sped up again. There was no denying it, the doctor was a handsome man, tall and lean, with a well-muscled chest and arms, as she had just lately come to learn. He had dark brown, slightly wavy hair and an unfashionable, neatly trimmed beard, complimented by a straight nose and slate grey eyes that ought to have been cold but weren't in the least. In fact, they held a distinctly warm light as they rested on her and made her uncomfortably heated.

"Why are you visiting the O'Donnell's?" she said, desperate for a safe topic of conversation. Dwelling on the doctor's manifold charms was a recipe for disaster.

"Let me see," he said staring ahead and counting off items from an invisible list. "Mrs O'Donnell is expecting again. I believe there is an earache in one, a scratched finger in another, an assortment of other scrapes and bruises and at least one sore throat."

"Not another baby! That will make fourteen, if it lives." The O'Donnell's had been remarkably fortunate in the survival rate of their offspring, the lady having birth seventeen babes and only lost three to date. The presence of three sets of twins in amongst the brood accounted for some of the numbers. The eldest child, Matt, was twenty, followed by his sister, Matilda, eighteen. Hetty lost track after that, but she had seen all of them come into the world during her twenty-eight years as the vicar's daughter, some she had actually been present at the birth.

"Aye, I've offered them a contraceptive, but they will na have it. O'Donnell say's it's against their religion! Catholics!" He said shaking his head.

Hetty, her colour rising at the topic, swallowed and said, "but you're Scottish, aren't you a Catholic too?"

"Aye I was raised Catholic, but I dinna practice noo. Ye'll have noticed me in the pew in yer father's church aye?"

"Why do you no longer practice Catholicism, Doctor Thornton?" she asked genuinely curious.

"Let us say I've learned thing or two about religion in my travels, and I decided some of the tenants of the faith dinna sit weel with me. The prohibition on contraception bein' one."

"Then you have converted to Protestantism?"

"Nay I wouldna say that either," he said.

"Then why do you come to our church?"

"Weel, it's all the same God, isn't it? And I prefer the view in your father's church," he said with a smile and a distinct twinkle in his eye.

"You prefer the-" she stopped, flushing. "Am I to understand that you come to church to see me?"

"Aye lassie, is that so surprisin'? Yer by far the prettiest thing in the church, if not the entire village."

"Will you stop calling me lassie. I'm a grown

woman of eight and twenty," she said, ignoring the rest of his speech, which was complete nonsense. There were at least a dozen much younger and prettier girls in the village than her.

"Aye and I'm five and thirty. Forgive my plain-speakin' l- Miss Rooke, but I like ye. Yer a sensible woman. At least ye are when yer no wanderin' into paddocks with bulls in 'em."

Her heart sped up and she flushed, at a loss for words.

"This is no' the time or the place for wooin'," he said glancing round the paddock they were traversing, "but would ye be open to me speakin' with yer father? I'd like permission to court ye. That's still the way it's done in England, isn't it? I've been awa' a mite long and maybe things have changed?"

Quite breathless with shock, she stammered, "M-my father will have no objection, I'm sure."

"Aye lass, but will you?" He had stopped and pulled her round to face him taking one hand in his. "It's not escaped my notice that any time I've tried to flirt wi' ye, yer've backed away in fright. I take account of maidenly shyness but yer not a girl, but a woman grown. The fact yer still no' wed, suggests to me that either every man in the county is a blockheid, or ye've chosen not to marry. Which is it?"

She gaped at him, her heart thudding. *It was as if he had delved right into her heart and laid bare her secrets. Yet he couldn't know her secret shame, the reason she had shunned all opportunities to marry.*

. . .

THE WAY her face blanched made him think he'd gone too far with his plain speaking. But he wasn't a man to beat around the bush and one month's acquaintance with the lovely Miss Hetty Rooke had been enough to seal his fate. It was ironic that he'd travelled all over the world and not met a single woman to bowl him out, yet one look at Miss Hetty's fair countenance had set him back on his heels in nothing flat.

To be objective about it, she wasn't the most beautiful woman in the world, but something sweet and compassionate in her gaze had snared him from the first. Further acquaintance had confirmed the first impression. She was kind-hearted, hardworking and intelligent, she took her duties to her father's parishioners seriously and spent her days attempting to lighten their burdens. She had an insatiable curiosity for knowledge and was a willing audience for his tales of adventure.

She was tall for a woman, which made her the perfect height for him, with dark blonde hair and eyes of a peculiar turquoise hue, her mouth was a mite too wide for beauty, but her skin was milky smooth, and she blushed delightfully. Her figure was slender, but her breasts curved generously for her frame. And her scent, something of patchouli and lavender, drove him crazy.

He had hesitated to act on his feelings, knowing that he might have to flee at a moment's notice, it was a cursed inconvenient time to fall in love, *but then when would be a guid time?* But continued proximity to his heart's desire and in particular the felicity of holding her in his arms in that mad dash across the paddock, had addled his brain. The words tumbled out before he could think better of them.

His heart pounded heavily in his chest as he waited for her response. She looked like a deer confronted with a hunter. He cursed his too direct speech. He'd spooked her. She was like a wild horse needing to be coaxed, and he'd blundered. What made her so skittish he couldn't fathom, but some experience in her past had made her wary of men. He'd like the opportunity to punish whoever was responsible.

"Are you serious Doctor Thornton?"

"Aye I am. I dinna joke about things of this nature Miss Rooke. Are ye willin' to get to know me better?"

She swallowed visibly, took in a breath as if about to be submerged in water, and nodded. Relief and a kind of euphoric joy filled his chest. *He hadn't won her yet, but she'd no' repulsed him.* A grin broke out on his face.

"Thankee Miss Rooke, I'll speak to yer father as soon as maybe." He kissed her hand and tucking her arm in his, resumed their walk up the hill to the O'Donnell's homestead.

CHAPTER 2

*M*erlow made good on his promise that afternoon, finding his waiting room empty by three o'clock he put up the closed sign on the door and escaped before another patient could materialise.

It was a pleasant summer afternoon, with a warm breeze and bright sunshine, that made him quite hot walking briskly up the street to the vicarage. He couldn't traverse the length of the village without being greeted by half a dozen people, and it was half an hour later before he finally pushed the gate open and walked up the path to the vicarage.

The door was opened by Mrs Corcoran, the vicar's housekeeper who smiled at him, wiping her floury hands on her apron and conducted him to the vicar's study at the back of the house. The room was cluttered with books and papers on every available surface and the man himself was seated at a large desk under the window, with a prospect of the back garden, where flowers bloomed in abundance and a trellis vine threatened to invade the house.

Looking round distractedly, Mr Rooke pushed his spectacles up his aquiline nose and scrubbed at his wispy fair hair mussing it further. "Thornton my dear chap!" He rose holding out a hand in greeting. "Tea, Mrs Corcoran, if you please."

"Am I disturbing you?" Merlow asked waving at the chaos of papers and books on the desk.

"Not in the least. I'm glad of the distraction. Sunday's sermon is being most recalcitrant."

Mrs Corcoran went away to fetch the desired tea and the vicar moved a pile of books so that Merlow could sit down in the other chair.

Reseating himself, Mr Rooke said with a smile, "what can I do for you? Or did you come to see Hetty? She's up at the church, the ladies committee or some such. I think they are planning the church fête."

"Nay I came to see you sir," he said with smile. "Although it is on Miss Rooke's account that I'm here."

The vicar raised his eyebrows, but before he could ask, Mrs Corcoran came in with the tea tray, and it was several minutes before the conversation could be resumed, what with the serving of tea, cake, biscuits and pleasantries.

Once Mrs Corcoran withdrew and Merlow had helped himself to another slice of fruit cake — he had missed lunch– Mr Rooke prompted him. "On Hetty's account?"

"Aye." Merlow swallowed a sustaining mouthful of strong, sweet, black tea and felt himself flushing slightly. "I wished to ask yer permission to court your daughter sir. I'm mighty taken with her. In fact, I'm fair smitten," he admitted frankly.

Mr Rooke blinked his pale blue eyes a moment and then smiled. "Well, I'm very glad to hear that Thornton and I appreciate your candour. But I must tell you that there have been several men before you who have all failed miserably to persuade her to have them. But I wish you every success my dear chap."

"Then you've no objection sir?"

"None at all! I'd be delighted to see her happily settled."

"Thank ye sir. I will certainly hope to be more persuasive than my predecessors. Have ye any notion as to why the lass has refused them?"

Mr Rooke shook his head. "She seems to have this absurd notion that she cannot leave me to fend for myself. But it's nonsense as I've told her. I would simply increase Mrs Corcoran's days to five instead of three and hire another girl from the village to help her."

Merlow nodded thoughtfully and dunked and chewed a ginger nut biscuit. "Weel the lass hasna encountered Scottish stubbornness yet. I mean to have her to wife eventually. I flatter mysel' she's noo indifferent to me. It's a guid thing I'm a patient man." He finished his tea and set the cup down. "You needn't be worrit I'll force her tho, ye ken. I've a might more address than that. She'll come to no harm at my hands sir I give ye my word. She's a fine lass, kind and dedicated, she'll make an excellent doctor's wife. But more than that, I love her. I can only hope to persuade her to return my regard."

The sound of a door closing and footsteps on the wooden floorboards followed by a "Papa?" and the door, which was ajar being pushed open, revealed Hetty. She stopped at sight of Merlow and flushed. "Doctor Thornton."

He rose with her father at her entrance and nodded to her with a grin, his heart lifting at the sight of her. "Miss Rooke," he stepped forward and took her hand. "I was just speaking with yer father on the matter we discussed this morning."

"Oh!" she coloured fiercely. "Papa?"

Rooke grinned. "Yes Hetty, Doctor Thornton has made a frank avowal of his intentions towards you and if you've no objection I am happy to encourage him. But in the end the decision is yours."

Her lips trembled and her smile wobbled. "Thank you, Papa." She turned her gaze back to Merlow and said softly, "I am flattered."

"But?"

"I think I've left a book in the parlour," said Rooke tactfully and left the room.

HETTY'S HEART RACED. "W-what did you say to him?"

Merlow squeezed her hand and said gently, "that I love ye lass and wished to court ye right properly. If ye'll permit me?"

"You hardly know me-" she protested weakly, her knees feeling ready to collapse and her head spinning.

"I know enough. In fact, I knew within minutes of clapping eyes on ye that I wanted ye somethin' fierce. Since then, I've observed ye going aboot yer business with the parishioners, how much ye care fer them. I've seen ye deal tactfully and compassionately with those who have lost loved ones, hold yer head in a crisis and dispense practical help to those in need, comfort distressed children, aid the elderly and deal patiently and effectively with the politics of the lady's committee.

"I canna sleep for thinking aboot how much I want te kiss ye and hold ye in my arms. Ye've got me fair addled love." As he spoke, he eased an arm round her waist, pulling her against him and cupped her cheek in one hand, tilting her face up towards his. His grey eyes, that ought to be cold, glowed with an inner fire that liquefied her body and robbed her lungs of air.

She put a hand on his chest to stay him, yet unaccountably found her fingers curling round the lapel of his jacket as if to sustain herself upright, for her legs felt awfully wobbly. Her lips parted to say something, though she hadn't a clue what and then his mouth descended on hers in a tender caress, that took the remaining breath from her body and sense from her head.

The tingling rush of pleasure his mouth created against hers, made her dizzy and she pressed closer against the solid warmth of his body for fear of collapse. His arm tightened round her, cinching her closer and his lips wreaked havoc with her senses, gliding gently over hers and drawing an answering pressure from her. The strength of his arm supporting her and the gentle tingling warmth of his mouth on hers, drew a soft noise of involuntary delight from her throat.

Hetty had been kissed before, but not like this.

Her previous experiences had been less than pleasant, but this... set her pulses racing and liquefied her body. She became acutely aware of the shape and heat of his form pressed so tightly against hers and the rigid outline of something hot and hard behind the fall of his breeches. She knew perfectly well what this was and what it indicated. She ought to be terrified. But his lips continued to coax such delightful responses from her, and these overrode her instinct to pull away and flee from the imminent danger of his arousal.

When his tongue passed gently along the seam of her lips and probed her mouth with equal gentleness, she lost her head entirely and tilted her face to aid his access and responded with another little noise of surrender. She was clinging to him now with both hands and pressing her body closer, offering her mouth for his delightful teasing lips and tongue to plunder. Her senses were drowning in an intoxicating mélange of pleasurable sensation.

MERLOW LIFTED HIS HEAD RELUCTANTLY, breaking the kiss that had his senses swimming, his cock hard as an iron bar and hotter than a blacksmith's forge, his breathing elevated and his pulse thundering.

"I knew it," he murmured, his eyes devouring her flushed cheeks, slumberous eyes and plumped lips. "It's a rare thing lass, this kind of connection. You'll not deny you feel it too?"

She blinked as if dazed, then shook her head as if to clear it. "I've never experienced a kiss like that," she confessed. Her voice husky and low, sent a pulse through his body and his hands tightened on her involuntarily. He wanted to kiss her again, devour her, but something in her eyes stayed him.

"I hope that is a compliment," he said reaching for humour to lighten the mood, the shadow in her eyes was worrying him.

She lowered her lashes, dipping her head forward slightly, hiding her expression. "I cannot–it was unwise-"

He lifted her chin to see her face. "What -"

She pulled away from his touch, pushing against his chest with her hands, and he let her go reluctantly, a sick feeling settling in his stomach.

"Your attentions are flattering," she said, smoothing her skirts with nervous passes of her hands. "But I cannot– you would be better not to-" she shook her head turning away biting her lip. Her distress was palpable and alarmed him far more than her disjointed words, which made little sense.

"Lass, what have I done to distress ye so?"

She shook her head moving towards the door, which for the sake of propriety was still ajar. "Please don't, I cannot -"

"Nay lass!" he reached for her, pulling her back against him, wrapping his arms around her middle and resting his face against her hair. "Whatever it is, it doesn't matter half as much as ye think it does. I'll not push ye. I'll wait until yer ready to tell me. But don't run from me. I'll not hurt ye I swear. Ye've nothing to fear from me Hetty I give ye my word."

"I cannot-" She whispered hoarsely. "Please do

not press me!" She pulled out of his embrace, and he let her go as she fled the room.

He let out a slow breath and rubbed the bridge of his nose reflectively. He had a fairly good notion what was going on, but how to win her trust sufficiently to get her to confess the truth?

He wondered grimly who was responsible, and he knew a moment of incandescent fury at the thought of her suffering. Whoever he was, he wanted to murder the son of a besom.

He sighed and picking up the tea tray took it to the kitchen for Mrs Corcoran, whom he found pressing our rounds of pastry for tarts on the big kitchen table.

"Where would you like this?" he said with a smile.

"Oh, Doctor you don't need to be waiting on the likes of me!" she said flushing. "Put it over there, Elsie will attend to it when she comes in."

"Tell me Mrs Corcoran, do ye know what things Miss Rooke is partial to?"

"What do you mean Doctor?"

"Her favourite colours, scents, flowers, foods, that sort of thing?"

"And what would you be wanting to know that for?" she said with a saucy knowing look to which he just smiled. "Well, let me think…" she said, wiping floury hands on her apron.

HETTY REACHED the sanctuary of her bedchamber and shut and locked the door, leaning against it as she attempted to stifle the sobs choking her throat with her hand.

His kisses had undone her, so tempting, so delicious... How she longed to surrender to what he was offering. But she could not. She could not lie to him. The prospect of watching his esteem fade away and be replaced by disgust, made her heart clench in her chest. *Could she bear it?*

She must tell him the truth before things went any further. Shame made her sink down on the bed, her head in her hands. She was such a fraud. The saintly vicar's daughter, when she was a fallen woman underneath. And no matter how many good deeds she did, it could not expunge her fall from grace. It would destroy papa if he knew and if Seb ever found out... She shuddered. How could she confess after all these years? She had told no one, except God to whom she had pledged her soul in redemption for her sin.

CHAPTER 3

*M*erlow found Hetty frustratingly elusive in the following days. He was pretty damned busy himself with his daily routine of training and meditation, patients in the surgery and paying house calls, but even so he made the time to try to call on her, but each time he did, he was met with the intelligence that she had either just stepped out or wasn't at home to visitors.

After four days of this he managed to ascertain that she was in the church hall running the church fête committee meeting, and he headed there.

The committee was made up of five members including Hetty, Mrs Sarah Craig a comely widow in her forties, Mr Beatson a man in his early fifties, the owner of prize-winning Fred, and the Misses Fielding, elderly twin sisters. They were all sat round a table in the hall drinking tea, when he entered from the vestry which connected the hall to the church building itself.

He approached the table with a smile and a nod. "Guid afternoon ladies, Beatson."

"Why Doctor, how nice to see you," twittered Miss Amelia Fielding. "Doris it's that nice young doctor," she said to her sister, sotto voce.

Doris Fielding snapped, "I can see that Amelia, I'm not blind!"

"Nice to see ye too Miss Amelia," he said warmly. Miss Amelia Fielding was technically the younger of the two women. Both of them had birdlike frames, white hair, and thin papery skin. "Miss Fielding," he said taking Doris' hand and kissing it with old-fashioned courtesy. "I trust the ointment I supplied for ye rheumatism has been effective?"

Doris blushed and said gruffly, "yes it has, thank you Doctor."

"Whatever are you doing here, Doctor?" asked Mrs Craig, with an arch smile.

"I came to see if I can be of help to the committee. Running a fête involves a mite of work, to my way of thinking. Can I be of service to ye Miss Rooke?" he asked turning towards Hetty and raising an eyebrow.

Hetty flushed, which wasn't lost on either him or the company, as he caught a nudge from Amelia to Doris's ribs out of the corner of his eye.

"That is very kind of you Doctor Thornton, but I don't think-"

"Nonsense!" said Mrs Craig robustly. "We can always use another pair of hands, can't we Alfred?"

Beatson, visibly kicked under the table sat up and said, "Certainly we could."

"Excellent!" he said drawing up a chair and sitting down.

"Tea Doctor?" said Mrs Craig pouring him a cup.

He accepted the tea and smiled at Hetty over the cup. She pressed her lips together and averted her eyes. Clearing her throat she said, "I believe the next order of business is the entertainment."

MUCH TO HETTY'S ANNOYANCE, at the end of the meeting, the committee dispersed except for the doctor who stayed to helped her put away the chairs and wash up the cups.

"There is no need, really," she protested. "I can manage."

He ignored her and went on helping, keeping up a running patter on the O'Donnell's latest crop of injuries and illnesses.

With the cups washed, dried and put away, Hetty held out her hand with a determined smile, "thank you Doctor I'm sure you must be busy, I won't keep you any longer."

He smiled and took her hand, "I'll escort you back to the vicarage."

She panicked then, her heart rate accelerating rapidly. *The dratted man wouldn't take no for an answer. What could she do to put him off?*

"I'm not going back to the vicarage just yet; I promised the Carson's I would look in on old Mrs Carson and make sure she was managing since she had that fall."

"I saw her this morning, she is doing quite well, but by all means let us go and see her again, she will love the company."

She sighed audibly, and he said, "ye won't get

rid of me that easily, Miss Rooke. I told ye I meant to court ye. Did ye think I wasna in earnest?"

"And I told you that I couldn't! It is most ungentlemanly of you to persist when I made it clear-"

"Your words were clear, but your kisses told me something else, Hetty," he said drawing her closer with an arm round her waist. He pushed up her chin with a finger and her eyes snagged on his lips outlined by the neat brown hair of his beard. She recalled the feel of it, ticklish and soft. And the tingling heat his lips aroused in her body. She pulled back, that panic licking at her again. She put her hands on his chest, her cheeks scalded.

"No!" she said quite forcefully, and he immediately let her go. She turned away. "I'm sorry Doctor Thornton but I cannot! I beg you to forgive me for leading you to think that your kisses would be welcome. My only excuse is that my brain was addled at the time. You must know that you are an attractive man, I-" she swallowed willing the tears clogging her throat not to burst forth. "I behaved inappropriately. I'm sorry."

"Nay lass." She felt his hands rest lightly on her upper arms and the warmth of them soothed the cold lump in her stomach. *Oh, the temptation to give in and let him...*

"I understand more than ye think, sweetheart." His words, murmured softly beside her ear, made her shiver and an ache of longing bloom in her chest. *Oh, to be able to take his words at face value.* But she knew better than to believe what a man said when he wanted her body, and the doctor had made it clear he wanted her.

He pulled her gently back against him, wrapping his arms across her middle and hugging her to him, his face rested against her hair. "Lass did ye no hear me properly the first time? I love ye. I'm offering ye marriage, not some casual roll in the hay."

She closed her eyes, her heart clenching and the sobs rising in her throat. *This was anguish. To have him offer her everything she wanted and not be able to accept... for if she did, and he discovered, as he inevitably would, her fallen state, she would see the love he professed fade from his eyes to be replaced by revulsion and contempt. She couldn't bear it.*

She stifled the sobs and shook silently in his arms, the tears rolling slowly down her cheeks. "Ah lass I didnae mean to distress ye so," he said turning her in his arms and hugging her close. "I wish ye'd see ye way clear to confide in me."

She shook her head.

Above her head he said softly, "I've nay earned ye trust yet. But I will." He rubbed a hand up and down her back soothingly. "I'll tell ye this lass. If I had him in my hands, I'd murder him for hurting ye."

She pushed back to look up at him startled. "You wouldn't!"

"I would." The grimness in his tone and expression made her shiver and she realised how little she knew about this man who professed to love her.

MERLOW, watching the change in her expression, kicked himself. The last thing he intended was to frighten her. *If she knew what he was capable of... she would truly run from him in terror. But that was all behind him now, he'd eliminated the men who were chasing him, hadn't he...?*

He cupped her face in his hands. "I've frightened ye lass and that wasna my intention. I'm Scots ye ken. Where I come from a man's no a man if he canna defend his women folk and bairns." He smiled ruefully. "If ye think I'm a might fierce ye should meet my brother Col. He's Laird Mac Sceanchain now that our father's passed on. The old man always said I was a stain on the escutcheon because I chose to pursue medicine over such manly activities as fighting, carousing and womanising. At times I think he thought I was a changeling and no son of his."

"Medicine is a noble profession," she said stoutly.

"Aye it is, and I knew it was what I wanted to do from the age of twelve. But it didn't go down well with the old man. Fortunately, I wasna his heir so there was little he could do to stop me, beyond trying to make me feel like I wasna his son."

"Did he disown you?" she asked indignantly.

"Nae he didna go that far, but he teased me unmercifully, called me names and suchlike, trying to shame me into being what he thought was a proper man. It bothered me a lot a growing up, but it doesna now. Fact o the matter is I'm as stubborn he was, the old foggit. Once I made up my mind, nothing he could say would make me change it. He gave up in the end. I like to think that maybe somewhere in his grizzled old heart he was proud o me.

But I'll never know, he passed away while I was still in China."

"Do you miss him?" She pressed her hand against his chest and a little flutter of warmth filled it at the gesture. He wanted to cover her hand with his but was afraid to in case he spoiled the moment, and she pulled away.

"Yes and no. He wasna an easy man ta live with ye ken. Mother died many years ago and it was just the three of us males knocking round the house together. In some ways my brother had the harder road to hoe, he couldn't escape like I did."

"Is your brother married?"

"He's a widower with two sons of his own. So, it's still an all-male household. He's three years older than me and right set in his ways now. He took it hard when Catriona died. I doubt he'll marry again."

"Thank you," she said quietly.

"What for lass?"

"For telling me about your family."

"I'm an open book Hetty. Ask me anything you like, and I'll answer it." *But would he really? Would he tell her about the three Chinese warriors who would never see their home again?*

She flushed and pulled away. "I had best be going, we have tarried here far too long."

"The Vicarage or Mrs Carson?"

"I should see Mrs Carson; I promised I would."

"I'll take you then. The old lady will be tickled pink to see us both. And think herself right important to get two house calls in one day."

"I can't get rid of you, can I?"

"Nae that ye can't."

He was right. Mrs Carson was tickled to get a visit from them both and nothing would satisfy her but that they take tea and biscuits with her. So, they stayed for tea and chatted, and then he walked her back to the Vicarage.

He wanted to take her in his arms and kiss her, but he couldn't do that on the vicar's front doorstep in full view of the entire village. So, he made do with kissing her hand and bad her good night.

Wending his way back to his house he reflected that he hoped she would sleep better than he did. Dreams of Hetty had a habit of disturbing his sleep. And grimmer ones could jerk him awake in a cold sweat when he thought about those warriors buried in a ditch just outside Oxford.

CHAPTER 4

The three Chinese men had been tailing him since he left Fife. In fact, they were the reason he left Fife in the first place. They had bailed him up in the Glen near his family home, the seat of the Laird Mac Sceanchain, when he was returning on horseback from a visit to a neighbour, whose wife was poorly.

The mist was starting to rise among the trees, as the sun was setting, and three Qing soldiers dressed in quilted blue armour lined with metal and studded with nails stepped out of the heather and gorse to block his path. Merlow immediately recognised the distinctive surcoats and over-trousers of the Qing agents, how they had tracked him to Scotland he didn't know. Why, he had an inkling of, and could only hope the manuscript and waidan sword, gifted him by his Master Zhanghu-Zi were safe where he had stashed them. That the Qing Government's fanatical desire to wipe out adherents of the Baguadao and eradicate the practice of Neidan had caused them to send agents half-way round the globe to do it, seemed incredible to him, but here they were.

Three of them and one of him. His fighting skills were good, but not that good, at least he didn't think so. His only advantage was that he was mounted, and they were on foot. If they dragged him off the horse, he was going to be in trouble.

The central man stepped forward, he was older than the other two and sported a long beard and moustache. He addressed Merlow in Nanjing Mandarin, the dialect he had learned while in China.

"Yang gui zi!"

White Devil

"You have something that belongs to us."

Making a split-second decision, Merlow kicked his horse hard in the ribs and charged forward. His only hope was to outrun them. The horse barged forward. The two younger men leaped at him as the horse shouldered through, knocking the lead man off his feet. One grabbed his leg, the other the stirrup on the other side. He kicked out with his feet to dislodge them as the horse continued forward, but hampered by the weight of the men. The one who had hold of his leg tried to pull him from the saddle, all the while yelling abuse at him in Chinese. The other tried to use his grip on the stirrup to mount the horse.

Gripping the horse with his knees to stay in the saddle, Merlow took a deep breath, exhaled, focused and chopped sideways at the man clinging to his leg, getting him across the throat. The man choked and let go, falling to ground. With the other one, he chopped at the point under the jaw adjacent to the ear. The man let go with cry of pain as his eyes rolled back in his head and he fell into the road unconscious.

Merlow urged the horse forward, and now free of the additional burden, he broke into a gallop leaving the men behind. Merlow looked back briefly, his heart thudding and saw the older man tending to the unconscious man. That blow could have been fatal, he hoped fervently it wasn't.

He rode hard all the way back to Sceanchain House. Emerging from the forest of trees that surrounded the Park and riding past the double-story, bow-windowed frontage of the stone-built mansion to the stables, behind and to the west of the main building, to dismount and rub down the horse.

Heading into the house via the rear entrance from the stables, he went in search of his older brother Col, Laird Sceanchain. He found him in the library behind a large mahogany desk, surrounded by papers, with a whisky at his elbow and a rough-coated terrier and a deer hound at his feet. A fire crackled cheerfully in the grate. Of his nephews there was no sign.

"Col," he said entering the room.

"Aye Merlow, want a dram?" he asked indicating the whisky.

"Thankee," Merlow agreed. "I'll get it," he said crossing to the sideboard and pouring himself a drink, bringing the decanter to top up his brother's glass.

"How fares Elspeth Munro?" asked Col leaning back in his chair and propping his feet on the deer hound's back. The animal didn't seem to mind.

"Nothing that some good food and bed rest won't fix. Where are the boys?"

Col sighed wearily. "Up to mischief nae doubt. They'll appear when dinners served, they have an uncanny knack for it." He stretched his neck, his long reddish hair falling round his shoulders, having come lose from its ribbon. "What do ye want with them?"

"I'll be leaving early tomorrow first light."

"Aye? I thought ye were going to bide a we bit?"

"I was," Merlow had considered telling his brother the truth but decided against it, principally because his brother's tolerance for his medical training was borderline, he would not understand Merlow's involvement in the Baguadao nor why he would put himself in danger to protect an ancient and sacred Chinese text. "I received a letter this morning from a colleague in England. He's invited me to a medical symposium in London, I thought I'd go." He said extemporising freely.

Those Qing men were dangerous, and while Col was well capable for taking on a standard fight, Merlow worried that the techniques used by trained martial artists would be beyond him. He also didn't wish to place his nephews in any danger. Like curious cats they would likely approach rather than flee from such a curiosity as a posse of Qing soldiers.

"Harrumph!" Muttered Col sipping his whisky.

"I'll come back," said Merlow, mildly, feeling a twinge of guilt.

He spent a restless night listening for the men trying to break into the house and rose before dawn to pack his single bag, take a small package of food and drink for the journey and saddle his horse. He was away from the house before the sun broke the horizon.

He followed the coast road of the Firth of Forth towards Edinburgh, crossing at the narrowest point by ferry and doubling back to Edinburgh. He had reached the Scottish border with England at Gretna before he spotted his Qing hunters, but he had been conscious of them the whole way, just hadn't sighted them. The itchy feeling their presence gave him disturbed his sleep and his digestion and he found it difficult to concentrate on his daily practice of meditation because of it. He could feel himself unravelling under the constant surveillance.

He crossed the border and made it to Carlisle, where he decided to confront them. But they proved elusive, and he kept moving south, sticking to well populated areas and roads, figuring he was safest in environments with plenty of witnesses. His followers would stick out like sore thumbs in their outlandish uniforms and likely attract the kind of attention they wouldn't want from the locals.

It was several weeks later, just outside of Oxford that the confrontation came. His horse had lost a shoe, and he was forced to lead him, it was coming on dusk and the strip of road he was on was deserted and bordered on both sides by dense forest. He was weary from the strain of weeks of silent pursuit, never able to relax.

The fading light of dusk, cast elongated shadows across the deserted road as Merlow trudged forward, leading his weary horse by the reins.

The sound of a cart behind him on the rutted road, made him turn and he saw a man driving a pair of horses in a cart with a woman beside him. Merlow moved over to the side of the road to let them pass, but the man slowed his team and called out.

"Is your horse lame sir?"

"Lost a shoe," said Merlow.

"Ah you're in luck man," he said with a broad smile through his bushy red beard. He was a big fellow, with broad shoulders and muscular arms. "I'm a blacksmith," he said descending from the cart. "I've some shoes in the back and my implements. I'll have your horse shoed in no time." He advanced toward Merlow his large hand held out in greeting. "Mitch Stewart, is the name, this is my wife Maggie." The woman leaned forward in her seat and waved with a smile. She had brown curly hair and a round face, with merry eyes and a snub nose.

"Please to meet ye, Merlow Thornton," he said, taking the other man's hand. He bowed in the lady's direction. "Mrs Stewart."

He turned as Stewart came back to him with a horseshoe, some nails, a hammer and a file. "Let me take a look, which hoof is it?"

"Front left," said Merlow, keeping a hand on his mounts bridle in case he spooked.

Stewart patted the horse's withers and spoke softly to him. "Now then my fine fellow, I'm just going to examine your hoof. That all right with you?"

The horse huffed and flicked an ear.

"Here then," said Stewart producing a wizened apple from a pocket and offering it on his great work roughened palm. The horse took the offering and munched on it while Stewart picked up his hoof and examined the damage.

In a few minutes he had filed the hoof and affixed a new shoe with a few nails. "There, good as new," he said straightening and walking the horse to check its gait.

"Thankye vera much!" said Merlow smiling and offering his hand again. "Can I be of service to ye? I'm a physician."

"Are you now?" Mitch smiled broadly. "You hear that, Maggie? A doctor. You wouldn't be looking for a place to practice, would you?"

"I might," said Merlow cautiously.

"We're from Pinner, just heading home now. It's a small place, thirteen miles from London, attached to Harrow, you might have heard of that?"

Merlow nodded, he'd heard of Harrow, the school for gentlemen made the place famous.

"We just lost our doctor, retired to Brighton to be near his children. To my knowledge we haven't found a replacement yet. There's a house with a surgery and all available…" Mitch stopped, invitingly.

Merlow pursed his lips. It was tempting, but he really couldn't do anything until he got rid of these curst Chinese off his tail. And really if he was going to set up practice it ought to be at home. But then, was there anything there except Col and boys to hold him? He had little emotional attachment to the place. Its memories for him mostly painful.

"I'll think on it thankye," he said politely.

"You'll be right welcome I assure you," said Mitch. He put his tools away and got back up into his cart. "We'll press on, about to lose the light. We'll be staying at the Crown Inn in Oxford if you care to join us."

"Thankye," he said again, waving them off before he prepared to mount his horse, checking the girth and straps keeping his bags in place, including the waidan sword.

Suddenly, a rustle in the underbrush broke the silence, and Merlow's hand instinctively went to the hilt of the sword. He'd taken to keeping it handy on the road, in case. Three figures emerged from the gloom; their silhouettes sharp against the dying light. Finally, the confrontation he had been waiting for.

The three Qing soldiers, their faces obscured by the darkness, their movements fluid and precise, circled him like predators. Merlow's heart quickened as he recognised the threat they posed, was this to be the end of him? Here now on a deserted road in the middle of England, and all for a text and sword not of his own culture or heritage? But he had given his word to his Master, Zhanghu-Zi. This text was possibly the last of its kind in existence. If it was destroyed, priceless knowledge would die with it.

"White Devil," the leader addressed him again in Mandarin, his voice shook with fury, his control slipping. "Hand over the Neidan text and the waidan sword, and your death will be swift."

Merlow squared his shoulders, his brown hair ruffled by the evening breeze, compressing his mouth into a determined line. Focus. He'd avoided this confrontation for weeks. He could avoid it no longer; it was a relief in many ways. His fate would be decided here and now. "I will never surrender them to you," he replied in heavily accented Mandarin, his voice steady despite the adrenaline pulsing through his body. He breathed, bringing everything into sharp focus.

With a sudden burst of speed, the Qing soldiers lunged forward, their movements a blur of motion. Merlow sidestepped their initial assault with practised ease, his martial arts training serving him well in the face of such overwhelming odds.

The clash of steel rang out in the gathering darkness as Merlow parried blow after blow, his muscles straining with the effort. His opponents fought with a skill born of years of training, their movements fluid and precise, each strike aimed with deadly accuracy. Sweat dripped down Merlow's back under his shirt, his heart thudding hard but steady, all those hours of relentless training were paying off. With each exchange, he countered with a speed and agility that belied his muscular frame, his movements a graceful dance of steel and muscle.

As the fight raged on, the forest echoed with the sounds of their struggle, the rhythmic clash of blades punctuated by grunts of exertion and the occasional curse uttered in Mandarin. Merlow fought with a determination born of desperation, having begun he saw no way out of this but to keep going to the inevitable conclusion.

Finally, after what seemed like an eternity, Merlow saw his opening. With a swift, decisive strike, he disarmed one of his opponents, sending the Qing soldier staggering backward with a cry of pain.

The other two soldiers pressed their attack with renewed ferocity, but Merlow held his ground, his movements a blur of motion as he parried and countered with a precision and speed that left his adversaries reeling. He had found his stride, and he wasn't giving up without an almighty effort.

The older of the three soldiers came at him ferociously slashing with violent and relentless force, managed a slash at the man's torso with the sword, but it didn't stop his violent attack. Driven back, Merlow looked for a way to break through, conscious of the other men closing in to finish him off. He would be dead in seconds if he didn't do something drastic. He recalled a move his master had taught him. Ducking he rolled and sprang up to attack the older man in the rear, he went down with a kick to the back and Merlow delivered another blow that kept him down. Turning, he parried the other men and cut them down where they stood.

Merlow felt a surge of relief wash over him as he leaned forward to catch his breath. But it was short-lived as the older man rose slowly to his feet and stared up at him from eyes gone dark with the shame of defeat. A red stain spreading on his tunic from a wound in his side. *His blow must have found its target after all?*

"My soul is damned," he uttered in Mandarin, and he turned and ran into the gathering dusk, his shape was soon lost to sight. Gaping after him, it was a moment before Merlow turned his attention to the two younger men who lay bleeding on the ground at his feet.

Merlow watched stunned, as simultaneously, each of them reached with shaking hands into a pocket of their uniforms and took out something which they raised to their mouths.

"Deliverance by the elixir," they uttered and took the pills and bit into them. Their bodies stiffened in a rictus of pain and their eyes rolled back. They were dead in moments.

Merlow collapsed to his knees, tears wetting his cheeks as the pall of death encompassed him.

He knelt like that for a long time, lost to a dark place inside himself. Finally, he roused himself to drag the bodies off the side of the road into a ditch. He had no spade to bury them properly and the best he could do was cover the bodies with some soil and leaf mulch gathered by his hands.

He felt sick with horror for what had occurred. He had crossed a line he could never uncross. He was a doctor; he swore to save life, not cause death. And even though he hadn't delivered the fatal blows himself, he still felt responsible.

Was it worth it, to keep this sacred text safe if it caused such horrendous things to occur? What would his Master say of this development?

SOME TIME later he entered the Crown Inn and was hailed by Stewart seated at a table in the tap room with his wife.

"What happened to you man? We had quite given you up, we were about to retire to bed."

Merlow headed over to them, wearily. He still

felt sick to his stomach over what had transpired. He had looked briefly for the older man, but found no trace of him. *Would he survive that wound?* "I was—er—held up," he said vaguely.

"Sit down man, you look done in. Mrs Wakelin!" Mitch hailed the woman who proved to be the publican. She was in her forties with a generous figure and smiling eyes. "My doctor friend here needs a bed for the night, a meal and a drink!"

She smiled at him and said, "he shall have them, Mitch. Have you any news of my sister?"

"Aye she's well, and the babes too. Mrs Carson senior suffered a fall and is still poorly."

"I'm sorry to hear that, Mitch." She turned her attention to Merlow. "If you'll come sign the register, sir, I'll get a room ready for you." She turned and called over her shoulder to one of the serving maids, "Sally, fetch this customer a drink and an order of beef stew."

Merlow followed her to the desk in the entrance and signed the register.

"Merlow, that's unusual," she said inspecting his signature.

"Aye is Scot's ma'am," he said with a weary smile.

"You poor man, you look exhausted, come sit and Sally will fetch your victuals right promptly."

He found he was hungry in spite of the nausea, or perhaps because of it, and ate the thick meaty stew and fresh bread and cheese he was served, along with downing two pints of ale.

"So have you had time to think on my proposal?" asked Mitch, sipping his ale.

Merlow pushed his empty bowl aside with sigh. "Aye I have."

"And?" Mitch grinned encouragingly.

"I'd like ta accept yer kind offer, if the village will have me?"

"Have you? You'll be welcomed with open arms, I guarantee it. I'll introduce ye to the vicar when we get there. He'll see all is right for you. We don't have our own Mayor or Council. They reside in Harrow. The vicar is our Council representative."

"You'll be most welcome Mr Thornton," said Maggie with a smile.

CHAPTER 5

*A*fter completing his evening routine of training and meditation, Merlow was settling into a glass of red wine and a book before the fire in his sitting room, when a jangle of the front bell and a loud knocking on the door brought him to his feet rapidly. This was not unusual. People didn't just get sick in business hours, and he was often called out late at night to attend a patient.

He went rapidly to the front door and unlocked it to find Hetty standing there in a cloak and looking positively distraught.

"You must come quickly! It's Papa, he's collapsed!"

"Let me grab my bag love and I'll be right with ye," he said retreating to his compounding room to fetch his medical bag.

Closing and locking the door behind him, he strode out rapidly beside her. "Tell me what happened?"

"I found him collapsed on the floor of his study. He was burning up and has a rash. Mrs Corcoran told me she heard him coughing yesterday. I believe he has been poorly for some days, but he never said anything to me. I cannot believe I didn't notice and make him stay abed. He is always of the belief that soldiering on is the best course of action when one is ill."

"Was he conscious when you left him?"

"Yes, but he wasn't himself. He barely knew me. Mrs Corcoran was bathing his head. He was so hot-!"

"Hush love, we will see him right. I have some experience with treating fevers." They had reached the vicarage by this point, and she led him straight to the vicar's study. The room was as untidy as before and in the middle of the room lay the vicar with his head in Mrs Corcoran's lap while she applied a cool compress to his forehead. A bowl of water by her side.

"Well, what have we here Mr Rooke?"

"He keeps fading in and out doctor," said Mrs Corcoran. "He's hot as a forge!"

Just then there was a knock at the front door followed by it opening and voice calling, "Hetty-?"

Hetty turned and called. "We're in father's study, Seb!"

"I sent my boy to let him know, Miss Hetty," said Mrs Corcoran.

Hetty nodded as the big outline of her brother appeared in the doorway.

"What happened Het?" he asked.

"That is what we are just trying to ascertain, Mr Rooke," said Merlow, his eyes on his patient as he knelt beside him and began an examination.

Mr Rooke senior was indeed burning up. His

cheeks had a hectic flush, and he was breathing with rapid, shallow breaths that had an ominous rattle. His neckcloth had been removed and his shirt was open at the neck, showing an expanse of chest where a speckled rash of small red dots were visible between the sparse coarse hairs.

"We should get him into bed," said Merlow rising to his feet. "Mr Rooke?" he turned to the large man who was bending to lift his father easily. Mr Sebastian Rooke carried his father up the stairs to his chamber with the ease a smaller man might have shown a child. He looked nothing like his father or sister who were both fair and of slender build. Mr Rooke junior was huge and dark, with hair as black as soot and dark brown eyes.

Rooke's petite little wife was one of Merlow's patients as she suffered from a heart condition. The Rookes ran the local hostelry, The Bull's Head.

Depositing his father on the bed, Rooke helped Merlow divest the vicar of his clothes and get him under the sheets.

Merlow took out his glass thermometer and shook it before slipping it under his patient's armpit and holding his arm steady to keep it in place. Mr Rooke was restless and muttering, his eyelids fluttering. Mrs Corcoran, banished while they undressed the patient, had returned with another bowl of cold water and more cloths.

He checked the thermometer, as he suspected the vicar's temperature was dangerously high.

"I recommend ye cover his chest and head in the damp cloths, it is essential that ye get his temperature down."

"What ails him, Doctor Thornton, do you

know?" asked Hetty with trepidation as she wrung out a cloth and laid it over her father's torso. For decency's sake, the sheets covered his lower half.

"I think it may be typhus, lass," he said frowning.

"How could he have contracted that?" asked Rooke in his low rumble.

"I don't know, Mr Rooke, it might be best if you leave us, you wouldn't wish your wife exposed to risk."

"No, I wouldn't." Rooke's eyes widened in alarm.

"I suggest you wash thoroughly and fumigate your clothes before you approach your wife."

"Aye," Rooke nodded. "I might take Beth to stay with her sister until..." He chewed his lip. "Hetty, take care, I'm sorry to leave you with this."

"Go," said Hetty. "You must protect Beth, I understand."

He nodded and left, which made the room feel a lot less crowded.

Merlow packed up his bag and said, "keep applying the cold compresses and if you can, get a little water into him, he should keep up his fluids. I am going to see if I can prepare a concoction that will help. I suffered a similar fever in China and my teacher Zhanghu-Zi saved my life. I believe I have the receipt for it somewhere, I just have to find it. I shall be back as soon as I am able."

Hetty looked up distractedly and nodded. "Thank you."

"Don't thank me lass, I haven't done anything yet, and I may not be able to. But I'll do my best."

She smiled wanly and returned to her labour

over her father's body while he ran down the stairs and into the street.

Back in the surgery he spent the next two hours going through texts and notebooks looking for the elusive script. He had almost given up when he found it scrawled into the margins of a Chinese text.

It was a list of ingredients only, no quantities or proportions. He would have to guess those. Even assuming he had the requisite ingredients in his pharmacy.

He wrote out the list on a separate piece of paper and took it through to the compounding room and searched through his jars and drawers, canisters and pouches until he had assembled all the ingredients but one.

He glanced at the clock on the wall. It was approaching midnight. It would take him several hours to prepare the concoction. Leaving the surgery, he jogged back down the road to the vicarage and after a peremptory knock, let himself in and ran up the stairs calling out as he went so as not to alarm the women.

"It's me, just wanted to check on our patient." He appeared in the doorway. Hetty sat beside the bed, her father's hand in hers. He was still draped in wet cloths and breathing sluggishly. Mrs Corcoran appeared behind him with a tea tray, and he stepped into the room to get out of her way.

"I can't tell if he's worse or better," said Hetty.

Merlow stepped up to the bed and applied his thermometer again. After a few moments, he took the reading. "A degree cooler, that is good. Keep up the cool compresses. Have you been able to get him to drink anything?"

"A few sips only." Hetty swallowed. "Every now and then he seems to know me, but most of the time he is raving nonsense and quite difficult to keep still."

"It is the fever, lass. It's got into his brain and making him lose his sense. When ye get the fever down he'll be more himself."

"Have you anything you can give him?"

"Aye, I've found the receipt I spoke of, but it will take me several hours to prepare it. I just came back to see how you are faring before I make a start on it. If anything changes dramatically come and fetch me."

She nodded. "I will, thank you."

He gave her a sympathetic smile. "One of you should get some sleep so that you can relieve the other, he shouldn't be left alone in this state."

He left them then, returning to the surgery and his compounding room to begin the long process of preparing the mixture.

He wondered how he would approach this if Hetty were here with him? Would she be interested in the process? He surveyed his pile of ingredients on the compounding table and began to measure carefully the right amounts of each, working from his knowledge and memory of instructions from his master. He hoped that he was getting the quantities right.

Once he had a pile of the required items, he washed them carefully and laid them out to dry on a cloth, while he set a kettle to boil over the hearth.

He added the ingredients one by one to the

boiling water, covered the pot and noted the time. It was important not to overcook the herbs. After a few minutes, he removed them from the heat and left them to steep.

The mixture would require three decoctions of at least 45 minutes each to get the maximum benefit from the ingredients.

Pouring off the first lot of fluid which was a deep yellow-green colour, he added more boiling water to the pot and set it on the heat once more, repeating the process.

Three hours later, he had several large bottles of decocted herbal medicine, that he hoped would be effective in treating the vicar's fever and for anyone else who might need it.

HETTY HAD BEEN DOZING in the chair beside the bed when her patient coughed, and she sat up bleary-eyed. She blinked at the clock on the mantelpiece, it lacked five minutes to four, the sky was beginning to lighten outside. She had sent Mrs Corcoran to bed some hours ago. Her patient had settled between midnight and two, but had been restless in waves since then. Rising, she bent over him and murmured, "do you want a drink papa?"

She reached for the glass and lifted him forward to offer a sip. He blinked at her uncomprehending for a moment and her heart clenched. Finally, he sighed as if bringing her into focus. "Hetty!" he croaked and took a sip of the water she offered.

She settled him back against the pillows. His skin was still dry and hot but not so burningly hot as it had been. The worst of the fever seemed to come in waves.

She sat listening to his harsh breathing and tried to pray. He moved restlessly, muttering and the tears rolled silently down her cheeks. "Oh Papa!" she whispered. "Please don't die!"

She heard a noise below and started up, wiping her cheeks and went to the door. It was the doctor returned. He came up the stairs holding an amber coloured bottle in his hands and smiling.

"You, did it?" she exclaimed quietly.

"I don't know if it will help, lass," he said setting the bottle down on the bedside table and examining papa. "How has he been?"

"Restless in waves. I think his temperature is lower at the moment, but it can spike suddenly, and he becomes distressed and disoriented. That is when he doesn't know who I am." She wiped her cheek again and sniffed. The doctor very improperly squeezed her shoulder in comfort.

"Ye've done an excellent job of nursing him," he said. "Now let us see if this mixture can help make him more comfortable." He measured out a dose and said, "Lift him up, I'm going to tip it down his throat, it won't taste pleasant. He may gag and cough."

WHEN THEY HAD MADE Mr Rooke more comfortable, Merlow drew her to the door, away from her patient to say quietly, "the medicine should help to quiet him and treat the fever, but I can't pretend to ye that this is over yet. Typhus generally will take a while to run its course, the patient can be sick for weeks before the body throws it off, or succumbs. Most typically it lasts for around fourteen days and if the patient is going to succumb that comes early in the illness, but if the illness lingers and weakens them it can come later. I wish I had better news for ye lass."

She nodded, blinking back tears.

He wrapped his arms round her and held her close, kissing her hair gently. "Ye ken I'll do everything I can to save him, but I'm no miracle worker. That we will need to leave in God's hands, hmm?"

She leaned against him and nodded, her cheek resting on his chest.

"Now, one more thing," he said, holding her apart from him, so he could see her face. "Ye need to ensure ye get adequate rest and food, yersel', ken? Ye need to be strong to nurse him. Ye dinnae want to get sick too?"

"Yes, I understand." she said husky voiced.

"Good girl," he kissed her forehead. "We'll get through this with God's help, lass. I'll visit often to check on him, but it's likely there will be other cases, and I'll be needed elsewhere too. E'en so, if you need me, I'll come. If anything worries ye, send for me. I dinnae want ye fretting yourself unnecessarily. A trouble shared, is a trouble halved, ye agree?"

She smiled weakly blinking her eyes and clutched his hand. "Thank you. I don't know what I've done to deserve-"

"Ah, hush, lass. I love ye, remember? Did ye think those were hollow words? I'm a mite fond of him too for his own sake, he's guid man, but he's yer father lass, ye love him. I'd do anything to save ye pain."

She choked on a sob, burying her face in his jacket and he held her tight, stroking her back and wishing fiercely that bad things didn't happen to good people. After a bit, she pulled herself together, as he had known she would. She was a strong lass, and he eased his tight grip on her.

"There then, lass," he said, cupping her tear-streaked face. She had never appeared more beautiful to him than she did in this moment, her face pale, and tear blotched, her hair coming out of its bun. "I'll see ye in a few hours, let Mrs Corcoran take a turn nursing him and get some sleep. I need some mysel' or I'll be no use to anyone."

It was full daylight out the windows by now, they had both been up all night. He left her reluctantly, a kiss to her forehead and one softly pressed to her lips.

He got three hours sleep before the storm broke. Mr Rooke Senior was indeed not the only villager to succumb to the Typhus.

CHAPTER 6

*G*eneral Ming Liang paced the deck of the Junk, Shaolin, moored off a tiny Island in a channel of the foreign land called Scotland by its inhabitants.

He had thought himself so close to his life's goal when they arrived here in pursuit of the foreign devil who had spirited away the sacred text, just when he thought it was within his reach. Master Zhanghu-Zi had been tight-lipped to his last breath, but not so his lily-livered second-in-command, Cai Bo. The man had been glad to blab all about Zhanghu-Zi's foreign apprentice, gifted with the sacred texts to protect from the Imperial forces that threatened to destroy them. A man who would so betray his master, deserved to die a death with no honour, and Liang had given it to him.

But the knowledge Cai Bo had gifted to him, presented him with a dilemma of honour himself. As a General in the Qing army, he was honour bound to serve the directives of the Jaiqing Emperor, who had decreed that the Eight Trigrams

Sect Rebellion be stamped out and its sacred texts destroyed. But as a secret devotee of the White Lotus religion, of which the Eight Trigrams was a branch, he found his imperial loyalties in opposition to his personal beliefs, and the quest he had pursued his whole life. His search for the Elixir of Eternal Life. The key to which was said to reside within the sacred text called the Neidan or Golden Elixir. A text now in the possession of the foreign devil Sāng dùn or Thornton in his own language. The brother of the Laird Sceachain, a local Lordling of some kind. These foreign names and titles tangled his tongue, even though he had made a study of their peculiar language, English.

Thus, he abandoned his post, and fled with three of his faithful men, his apprentice Caishen, and his sister Aihan, in pursuit of the text. All the way to this Scotland.

The journey had been fraught with its own dangers, storms that threatened to capsize and destroy their vessel the Shaolin. A reluctant crew that just wanted to go home and was only prevented from rebelling and slitting their throats by the promise of great rewards upon arrival at their destination. With the continued absence of his men, every day that passed, brought more unrest to the disgruntled crew.

It was a fine sunny day today, a rare thing in this Northern climate even for this time of the year, Summer. He stopped his pacing and put the spyglass to his eye again in one more fruitless attempt to summon his men back from their assignment. But there was no sign of the small boat they had taken to the shore of the coastal village called

Dysart, where their target should have been residing.

"Nothing?" asked his sister, Aihan, behind him. He swung round to face her. She was a tiny slender reed of a woman, but he knew that was deceptive, trained like him in the arts of fighting, she was a lethal weapon wrapped in a beautiful package. Her long dark hair, slanted eyes and flawless skin, gave her the appearance of a renowned beauty, who could hold her own in the cut-throat court of the Forbidden City.

She was twenty years his junior and as much daughter as sister to him. He loved her fiercely and not for the first time regretted bringing her with him. But there had been no one to leave her with safely in the wake of his defection. She would have been hunted and captured by the Emperor's guards and probably tortured and killed.

"None!" he admitted, frustration tying his body in knots. "I must go myself to find out what has happened to them. They are my responsibility."

Aihan frowned. "Surely another week-?"

"No. I am done with waiting. I must seek them and the Neidan myself. I should have done this in the first place. It was wrong to send my loyal servants into a foreign land alone. This is my fault. I must rectify it."

"Let me come with you," she said laying a hand on his arm.

"Out of the question! I will not place you in any further danger. Besides," he lowered his voice for her ears alone, "if we both leave this crew will abandon us here. You must stay on board the Shaolin until I return."

She gave him a mutinous look and then nodded reluctantly.

"Good girl," he patted her comfortingly.

"Caishen!" He called for his apprentice.

Shang Caishen appeared, a young man of muscular build and handsome face who had served him as apprentice since the age of six. He was entrusted to Liang's care by Caishen's dying mother, the sister of a friend. He took the boy in as a favour to the man he owed his life to, and the boy had proven quick to learn and loyal to a fault. He was younger than Aihan by six years, but the two had been raised virtually as siblings.

He bowed. "Yes Master, how may I serve you?"

"I am going ashore to find Cheung, Ding and Zhou. And retrieve the Neidan. I have been remiss and should have gone myself. You will remain here and guard Aihan with your life, you understand?"

"Of course, Master Ming."

The General received his apprentice's bow to which he made one of his own and went below to change and ready himself for his journey.

DURAND PERCIVAL ARRIVED in Edinburgh six days after leaving the Prime Minister's office, having traversed the distance on the stagecoach via the Great North Road. He spent two nights in Edinburgh to recover from the journey and gather information about how to reach his destination. In the end he decided to dip into his expense account and buy a cob, a serviceable mare. If he was fortunate, he could sell it back for much the same price when he was done. The prospect of another five days of hell on a stagecoach returning to London didn't thrill him, he'd rather ride and take his time returning, once his mission was fulfilled. He could send a letter reporting his success after all.

He was unable to gather much information about his target, although Thornton's brother, the Laird Mac Sceanchain, which tongue twister he discovered meant son of Thornton, in English and was pronounced Skeehain, was known to come into Edinburgh on business occasionally. By all accounts he was a big, red-haired man known for his hard head and uncertain temperament.

Armed with all this knowledge he set out for Dysart and the ancestral home of the Laird of Sceanchain, in happy of anticipation of discharging his commission with all speed. Finding the property wasn't difficult, he came upon the double story, double fronted stone-built house with picturesque bay windows in the late afternoon. As it was summer, night fall was some hours way and the ambient temperature was still warm.

He dismounted in the wide driveway and approached the stone steps of the porticoed entrance, to knock on the large oak door, with its huge bears-head knocker. A bear featured on the escutcheon of the Thornton's coat of arms, he recalled from the information in the file Liverpool had provided him. Which spoke to the antiquity of the Sceanchain family, as bears hadn't roamed wild in England since the dark ages.

While he waited for someone to answer the door, he noted signs of neglect about the place, the gardens were somewhat overgrown, the paintwork round the windows was peeling and the mullioned windows needed a good clean.

When no one had come after five minutes, he knocked again, more forcefully.

"Haud Yer Wheesht!" came a male voice from within. A rattle of locks being undone, and the door swung wide to reveal a short, wizened man with a shock of grey hair falling in his eyes and an equally grey beard on his chin. He wore a loose shirt and leather waistcoat over grubby breeches. He squinted at Durand from watery blue eyes.

"Dè tha thu ag iarraidh?"

Durand stared at him helplessly. In Edinburgh he'd encountered enough Scots with passable English to get by, it hadn't occurred to him that he would find himself confronted by a non-English speaker.

"I wish to speak to the Laird Sceanchain." he tried.

"Aye, come away in," said the gnome of a man, holding the door wide.

"That yer nag?" he waved at the horse.

"Yes, it is."

He nodded and stepped out into the driveway and bellowed something in Gaelic. Which produced a young lad with auburn hair and freckles running. It became clear he'd come to take the cob to the stables, so Durand quickly unbuckled his valise from the saddle and accompanied the little old man into the house.

Wooden floors and stone walls hung with paintings, an assortment of weapons and heads of deer with enormous sets of antlers met his gaze. The furniture was old and heavy, everything had a feeling of permanence about it, as if it had the weight of history behind it and was proud of the fact.

The man reached a door on the right side of the hallway past the staircase leading to the second story and pushing it open, stuck his head through and said, "Sassenach to see ye mi Lord."

"What the devil?" *At least the Laird spoke English.*

Fergus held the door open and nodded him through. Stepping over the threshold he entered a dark wood panelled room filled with more of that heavy furniture and complimented by a worn red rug and equally worn red velvet curtains. The room was dominated by a large desk behind which sat a large read haired man–the Laird Sceanchain, he assumed. Two dogs, one large one small, lounged before the fireplace even though it was too warm for a fire.

"Who the hell are ye?"

Durand stiffened at the belligerent question and summoned his most affable smile. Setting down his bag he advanced with his hand held out. "Durand Percival, I believe I have the honour to address the Laird Sceanchain?" he hoped he got the pronunciation right.

"Hmph. Fine looking sprig, aren't you? " his host muttered, and rising from his desk came round it. "Aye ye do, what do ye want?"

"Actually, I'm looking for your brother Doctor Thornton."

"He's not here," he said flatly.

"Oh. I had understood he was staying with you?"

"He was. He left."

"When was that, pray?"

"Why, what do ye want with him?"

"I'm here on behalf of the British Government to offer him a commission."

His grumpy host looked at him under beetling red eyebrows and pursed his lips. If the man didn't sport such an horrendous scowl, he might be judged well looking, but it was difficult to see past the ill temper that had carved deep lines in his face and prematurely aged him.

"And what would the nature of this commission be?"

"The Government is about to launch a second Embassy to China; it is believed your brother could be of assistance."

"You want to send him back to that bloody heathen place? He just came home!" the Laird turned away and paced to the fireplace. Stepping round the dogs with more delicacy than his bad temper suggested he would, he came to a stop staring up at a portrait of a woman that hung over the fireplace. She was young and pretty and held a baby in her lap and a young lad within the circle of her arm. "He's been away for ten bloody years!" Durand doubted this statement was directed at him or required an answer, so he remained still and quiet. His host was visibly upset about something. Presumably his brother's long absence.

Finally, he turned back and said, "I can tell you he left here two months ago to attend a medical conference in London. He said he'd be back, but I've not seen or heard from him since. I suggest you seek him in London."

Durand sighed in frustration. *He'd come all this way for nothing?*

"Thank you," he bowed politely. "Can you tell me where I might find suitable accommodation for the night?" *A polite host would offer him a bed.*

"The Speckled Hen will accommodate ye," said his ungracious host.

Durand nodded stiffly. "I'll bid you good day then."

"Hmmp," was the mumbled response.

Picking up his bag, Durand headed back to the front door, let himself out and went in search of his horse, which he found munching on a bag of oats in the stables. Of the freckle-faced boy there was no sign. The cob had been divested of her saddle, so he was forced to re-saddle and bridle the mare, and reattach his bag before leading her out into the driveway and remounting.

He headed back towards the centre of the seaside village looking for The Speckled Hen, his normally even temper considerably ruffled by the rudeness of Thornton's brother. No wonder the doctor had decamped, a more curmudgeonly character he'd not had the misfortune to meet before.

BY DINT of stopping and asking for directions several times, he finally found the Speckled Hen hostelry. All the way there he had a taught feeling between his shoulder blades, that he put down to tension from irritability. As his arrival coincided with the serving of the evening meal, he found himself waved through to the stables and left to fend for himself. By now thoroughly out of temper, he was tempted to go elsewhere but the prospect of another hour in the saddle dissuaded him. With the mare sorted, he headed wearily across the courtyard towards the Tavern, the hubbub of conversation and the smell of food greeted him as he entered and made his way to the front entrance to secure himself a room and a meal.

Finding the counter unattended, he rang the bell and stretched his shoulders, rolling them and cracking his neck trying to dislodge the peculiar feeling he'd had between his shoulder blades since he left Sceanchain House.

Normally he'd be alarmed, by that feeling, as it usually denoted, he'd picked up a tail, but in this case, there was no reason for anyone to be following him. His mission was simple and not dangerous. Annoying as it had turned out, but not dangerous. He put the feeling down to stiffness from lack of exercise for several days. He needed to reinstate his daily exercise routine; it got shot to hell by the stagecoach trip.

The publican finally appeared and gave him a room; his request for room service was refused.

"Sorry we're a mite short-handed tonight. Ye can get a meal served to ye in the taproom." he said with scant apology.

Durand bit his tongue with exasperation. It would do no good to make a fuss over the poor service. Instead, he headed into the tap room to get a meal, ordering both a large serve of the stew on offer and a tankard of ale. Finding a seat on the settle near the fireplace, which, with the temperature plummeting rapidly outside, had been lit. He listened idly to the conversations going on around him. He was on the edge of dozing off from the heat of the fire, when a voice with a northern English accent, cut through the general buzz with the words "did you hear about the Chinese warriors terrorising the countryside?"

Sitting up with a jerk he looked around for the source of these peculiar words. Three men were seated at a table to his left and the man who had spoken, grinned when his companions shook their heads.

"Outlandishly dressed they were. In loose quilted blue garments like oversized tunics and pantaloons, with peculiar helmets on their heads and carrying swords."

"Where was this?" asked one of his audience.

"Right here in Fife! Lurking about in the underbrush, frightening passers-by they said. But when the constable went to find them, there was no sign of them."

"Banbury story!" scoffed one of his listeners.

"So, I'd I've thought too, but how do ye explain this?" he produced a piece of blue fabric from his pocket and laid it on the table. From this distance Durand couldn't make out more than the colour, but the other's comments confirmed it was quilted.

"Ye got that from a child's quilt!" exclaimed one of the men, poking it with a finger. "No sane man would get around in blue quilted garments! It's absurd!"

The conversation was cut off in the next moment by the appearance of a dagger, seemingly thrown with terrifying accuracy, pining the quilted fabric to the table. And a Chinese man of tall stature, well-built but not young, possible forty-five or more, it was hard to tell in the flickering light of the lamps and candles, appeared beside the table, leaning in menacingly.

"Uniform of Qing army is no laughing matter!" the man was dressed in shirt and breeches with a long leather coat over the top and a broad brimmed hat on his head.

The men at the table leaned back away from the menacing Chinese, visibly startled and intimidated.

"Where you get?" the Chinese asked the man who had produced the cloth.

"I got it from the man who told me the s-story," he stammered.

"Where *he* get it?"

"He was walking through the Glen one after-noon late, about two months back when these three Chinese bailed up a Scotsman on horseback. The Chinese were on foot. By all accounts the Scotsman was Doctor Thornton, the Laird's brother. They addressed him in their native tongue, and he responded in kind. They threatened him, but the doc wasn't afraid, he took them on, all three, and won!"

The Chinese man jerked at his statement and Durand saw his hands clench by his sides. But he said nothing, continuing to listen to the story as it unfolded.

"One of the Chinese was dragged several feet by the stirrup of the doctor's horse and that is when he lost part of his clothing. It was ripped off in the skirmish. The doctor rode off and one of the Chinese tended to the other two. When they could walk, they all sloped off. The fellow who told me all this, waited until they left before, he came out of hiding and took the piece of cloth as proof of what he had seen."

"When was this?" the Chinese asked tightly, his fists still clenched.

"According to the fellow, two months ago. By all accounts the doc left the next day, headed for Edinburgh. With the Chinese after him. They were spotted in Edinburgh several times I'm told." The tale teller seemed happy with this bit of information, perhaps because it added an epilogue to the story.

"You seem to know a lot about this," probed one of the other men.

The man had quite an audience now, the dagger having drawn attention, and he was clearly enjoying himself. The Chinese didn't appear to be so happy.

"Aye well once I had the initial tale, I was curious and followed up, there was lots of sightings of the Chinese around that time, but none now for several weeks. The last I heard the doc was headed south over the border, Carlisle, I think. Seems the Chinese went with him."

Durand's meal appeared at this point, and he was about to tuck into it when a kerfuffle at the taproom entrance made him look up.

A fellow staggered to the bar puffing for breath and announced in a carrying voice that cut across the babble of chatter "tha Sionach na laighe ann am meadhan na sràide agus tha e a' coimhead marbhtach."

"What did he say?" asked Durand, sitting up, as people began rising from their seats and the babble surged up again.

"There's a Chinaman lying in the middle of the street, and he looks mortal bad," translated one of the men rising with the Englishman that told the tale of the Qing soldiers. Durand's eyes clashed with the tall Chinese man who had so lately been interrogating the Englishman, he had heard the translation too and its effect upon him was shocking. He went pale and turned, pushing his way through the crowd, who were all surging towards the entrance, he exploded out into the street. Durand followed him abandoning his dinner with mild regret. As he fought his way to the entrance and into the street he saw the Chinese man, coat flying about him as he ran, hurtle down the street to the gathering crown at the next intersection.

Durand took off after him and reaching the crowd, pushed to get a better view as the tall Chinese dropped to his knees beside the body of a man in the middle of the road. The prone man was dressed as the Englishman had described, in quilted blue fabric studded with metal and by his features, he was also Chinese. There was an old bloodstain on his chest and his face was waxy pale.

The tall one leaned over him and addressed him, presumably in his native tongue. It sounded outlandish to Durand. The man, who lay on his back on the cobbles of the road, opened his eyes and said something back. It obviously cost him an effort and the other man held his hand tightly as he spoke. The conversation was short and as Durand watched the life drained from the poor fellow leaving his compatriot grim face, with tears trickling down his cheeks.

The tall Chinese, rose, gathering up his dead brethren and walked off with him much to the astonishment of the crowd. The light was almost gone by now and the crowd began to disperse heading back to their homes or the tavern. Durand went with them to resume his meal, listening with half an ear to the talk around him, some of it in Gaelic which he couldn't understand and some in English which he could, despite the thick Scots accents. It was all speculation and wonder, but nothing that was of any help to him in locating the elusive doctor Thornton.

Stifling a yawn, he gave up on the gossips and took himself off to bed, having a quick wash in the cold water provided, he couldn't be bothered ordering hot, and fell into bed. The mattress was comfortable, if a little soft, and the sheets good quality and freshly laundered. More than he had expected given the level of service so far extended.

He closed his eyes, wondering drowsily what he could do about Thornton and these pesky Chinese. He lost the train of his thought and fell asleep, to be jerked awake sometime later to the sensation of a blade on his throat and the outline of a man standing over him.

He stiffened and lay still, his heart thudding fast and all his senses on abrupt, high alert. *So much for this not being a dangerous mission.* He had a knife under his pillow but couldn't reach for it. *Really, he had been very careless.*

"What do you want?" he asked quietly, wondering if this was an opportunistic thief or something more sinister. *Had one of his past escapades, caught up with him?*

"You seek physician, why?" *The Chinese! This whole thing was turning into a damned coil!*

"Why do you want to know?"

"I ask questions!" the other man moved the knife closer, and he felt the sting of the blade pinking his flesh.

"I have a message for him, from the British government."

"Hm. I seek him too, we go together."

Durand stifled a groan. "Why do you want to find him?"

"My business!" The knife bit deeper and Durand felt the hot sticky drip of blood running down his neck.

"All right!" He put up a hand passively. "Will you give me your word you won't cut my throat in my sleep?"

The other man gave a single sharp nod. Removed the knife from his neck and bowed. "On my honour. But if you attempt to escape me, I will hunt you down and hurt you. Understood?"

"Understood."

"I sleep on the floor; we leave at first light."

Durand sighed and lay still, staring at the ceiling listening to the Chinese organise himself to sleep on the floor, taking out a bedroll from his pack and wrapping himself in it. *Did he know about the body in the ditch?*

"Good night, English man."

"Good night, Chinese," he responded, thinking

there was no way in hell he would sleep. He was wrong, listening to the other man's steady breathing he fell asleep and was awakened to grey dawn light by a shaking of his shoulder and a peremptory, "we go."

CHAPTER 7

*S*eb returned from depositing his wife Beth with her sister, to help Hetty nurse their father, and she was inordinately grateful for that. His calm, steady presence, and his physical strength, eased the burden considerably. She could rest easy when she left papa in his care, knowing he would do all that she would and more for the man who had raised them.

The fact that Seb was not papa's physical son made no difference in the bond between them and between Seb and herself. They shared a mother, and Seb, being four years older, had been her big brother all her life.

Five days after his collapse, the fever still wracked her father's body intermittently, weakening him by the day. Merlow's medicine helped ease the fever when it was at its worst, but it was no cure. She was mortally afraid every moment, that the battle would be lost, for how much longer could papa withstand this horrible fever?

Mrs Corcoran made him sustaining broths,

which they fed him between bouts of the fever and Merlow checked in several times a day between his other patients.

Taking a tray back down to the kitchen, after feeding papa a serve of broth and leaving Seb with him, she was about to turn her attention to the pile of well-wishes the parishioners had sent for her father, when a knock at the door sent her scurrying to answer it.

"Merlow!" she said smiling in relief at seeing him. She had long given up fighting the pleasure and comfort his presence brought, but on this occasion his expression dimmed her smile immediately. "What is it?" she asked, letting him into the house and leading him into the front parlour. She hadn't seen him since yesterday, which meant he'd been busy with another patient. He looked tired and pale and there was a shadow behind his eyes that made her heart clench.

"The O'Donnell's youngest." His voice broke and his face cracked.

"Oh no! Little Benjamin?" She said, a knife in her chest, tears started to her eyes.

"It all happened so quickly," he said his voice thick. "He threw the rash yesterday and his temperature climbed alarmingly. We tried immersing him in cold water, but the poison in his system was too much, his lungs too congested." He shut his eyes tight, but they couldn't disguise the tears that leaked down his cheeks.

She flung her arms round him in comfort, no thought in her head but to ease his pain by sharing it. "I'm so sorry!" she whispered, cradling his head against her shoulder, her hand on the back of his skull and wept with him. His arms held her tight against him. His tears soaked through her dress as he fought to regain control of his emotions, his face buried in her neck.

"Thank you," he said eventually. Letting her go so that he could wipe his face and blow his nose on a handkerchief.

She sniffed wiping her own face.

"I will go and visit the O'Donnell's tomorrow; they must be devastated. And I'll write to the Bishop in Harrow, ask if we can borrow the curate to run services while papa is ill. How long do you think this will go on for?"

"There have been four more cases overnight, that's ten including yer father and little Ben. And that's not the end of it, but the beginning, I think. We need to encourage those with little ones and the elderly to leave the village, until the worst is over. They are the most vulnerable. Healthy adults stand the best chance of surviving this scourge."

"You're right, what of the Misses Fielding and Mrs Carson? Where would they go?"

"I dinnae ken, perhaps yer brother can suggest something?"

"He's with Papa, let us go up and ask him."

She led him upstairs to her father's bedchamber where Seb sat reading a book by the light from the window, his big frame overflowing the armchair, his feet stretched out and the household cat, a round tabby named Daisy, curled up on his lap. She was one of the litter that Seb had rescued and brought with him and Beth from London.

Papa was sleeping, his breathing a little congested sounding but at least the fever had abated for the moment. She had no doubt it would spike again later that evening; it always did.

"Seb," she said softly beckoning him to the door. He moved the cat gently to the bed, rose and trod quietly for such a big man following her out into the hallway.

"Doctor Thornton has just advised me that the fever took Little Benjamin O'Donnell last night," she swallowed as her voice cracked, and wiped a tear off her cheek.

"No," rumbled Seb in consternation.

"I'm concerned ye ken that the worst is yet to come and we've a mite of vulnerable souls here, the elderly and the very young. If we were to send them away have ye any suggestions as to where?" asked Merlow.

Seb nodded. "Aye, Beth's sister and her husband will take them. She owns a tavern in London, and he has houses all over."

"Good." Merlow clasped Seb's arm. He turned to Hetty, "I'd best be getting on, take care of your patient and each other, I'll come back in a few hours. See if I can persuade the Misses Fielding to leave their house for a spell in London." Merlow kissed her cheek and headed downstairs before she could say more.

She watched him descend the stairs with a strange, heated ache in her heart. Since papa fell ill, she had ceased to try to keep him at arm's length, she needed his comfort for one thing, and it would make it awkward if she were to spurn his affections. She would have to deal with what to do next in the aftermath. For the moment all she could think of was the next hour, the next day. Nothing mattered except keeping papa alive.

She turned back to Seb and caught the questioning expression in his eyes.

She flushed. "You needn't look so Seb, nothing–nothing untoward has happened!"

"Aye, it had better not, or doctor or no, I'll string him up!" growled Seb.

"Papa gave him permission to court me," she said, her colour still high. "His intentions are honourable, I assure you."

"Good. Question is, are you willing to have this one?" Seb raised a dark eyebrow.

Her cheeks felt scarlet. It was a question she had asked herself a thousand times. She wanted to, oh how she wanted to, but she dreaded what would happen when she told him the truth. When he learned she wasn't the good girl he thought she was...

When she didn't answer, Seb patted her arm. "He seems like a good man, Hetty, on the surface a perfect choice for you. Do you know any ill of him?"

"No, none!" she said quickly.

Seb grunted and added. "I'll get Garmon to check into him. If there are any skeletons in his closet, Garmon will find them."

Garmon Lovell was Seb's employer and brother-in-law and from what Hetty could gather, both a powerful and wealthy man. She had only met him a few times and while he wasn't as solidly built as Seb, and in fact his appearance was quite assuming, with brown hair and hazel eyes, when he entered a room, you could feel the atmosphere change. He carried an aura of command that made the air around him crackle and the blank hardness behind his eyes, made her shiver with apprehension. Mr Garmon Lovell was not a man to cross.

A cough from the sick room sent them both back to their father's bedside.

THREE NIGHTS later Hetty was sitting with her father, Seb having left that morning with a carriage full of the most vulnerable, bound for London. Papa's fever had spiked again, and the medicine wasn't bringing the fever down as it usually did. The constant toll of the fever was making him febrile, and she was as worried as she had ever been, bathing him in wet cloths. She had him propped up with pillows to ease his congested breathing and around mid-night when his breathing became more laboured, she resorted to prayers. This reversal was a shock, because he had been brighter that morning, even able to converse a little and take leave of Seb before he left. But as the day wore on, he worsened rapidly and Hetty was terrified he had reached the end of his strength.

She was so absorbed in listening to his breathing and watching him she didn't hear the step on the stair and almost jumped out of her skin when the door pushed open and Merlow stood there.

"You didn't answer, so I came up," he said, advancing into the room. "He's worse?"

She nodded unable to speak for the constriction in her throat.

"His breathing is severely congested," he said after a quick examination. "Fetch me boiling water in a bowl and a towel."

She obeyed him without question. Coming back up with the bowl of steaming hot water and towel over her shoulder she entered the room to find he had propped papa up further with more pillows and set the feeding tray with legs over his lap to take the bowl. She set it down on the tray.

"I'm going to try some of this," he held out a vial of something to her, and she took a cautious whiff, it was strong and seared her nostrils, immediately making her head feel clearer.

"What is it?"

"Menthol. It is distilled from peppermint. It clears and soothes the air ways. I am hoping it will prove an effective decongestant for his lungs," he said putting several drops of the liquid in the steaming water. "Come and hold him, I need to get his head over the bowl and get him to breathe it in." She came and held her father as he instructed.

"Mr Rooke," he addressed his patient. "I need you to breathe as deeply as you can, do you understand me?"

"Mmm," Papa mumbled.

Placing the towel over papa's head and keeping his head over the bowl, Merlow spoke slowly, "breathe in... and hold... Breathe out slowly... Breathe in... and hold..."

Her father's breath rattled, and he coughed between breaths, but after a few minutes the coughing eased, and the ominous rattling sound subsided. He seemed to be breathing easier. She wiped the tears off her cheeks.

"Thank you!" she whispered to him over papa's head.

He nodded and eased papa back onto his pillows.

He produced another small pot and handed it to her. "You can apply some of this unguent to his chest, the fumes will help ease his breathing and keep his lungs clear." she took the lid of the pot, and the same pungent smell of the menthol assailed her nostrils, this time it was in a goose fat emollient.

"The fever didn't abate with the medicine tonight." she said with a worried look. "He's so frail, can he take much more of this?"

Merlow produced his thermometer and took papa's temperature.

"Actually, it's not as high as it's been before," he said.

"No? That is a relief, but the medicine didn't quiet him like is usually does."

"The ingredients are losing their efficacy as his body gets accustomed to them. I can increase the dose a little. Try giving him half as much again next time."

She nodded.

"Is he still taking nourishment?"

"Yes, he has soup three times a day, in fact he seemed better this morning, more lively and even able to talk a little, I thought he was on the mend." She wiped her face.

He wrapped an arm round her bringing her into his embrace.

"He is I think, not out of the woods yet, but I think he has turned a corner. He will just need to be carefully nursed, make sure he doesn't over tax himself. He is very weak and fragile."

"I know. He was always thin; he is skeletal now!" she said gulping on a sob.

Merlow kissed her hair, a gesture she found so comforting she nuzzled closer, wrapping her arms round his middle. Finally, she lifted her head to look up at him. "How are you holding up? More cases today?"

He sighed and rubbed his face. "Two more, I'm just grateful your brother was able to remove the most vulnerable today."

"I hope they haven't taken the infection with them."

"Provided they all fumigated their clothes and luggage before they left, they should be fine. It's not transmissible through close contact, as far as I can ascertain."

"What causes it then?"

"I can't prove it, but I suspect it is caused by a bite of some small insect, flea, bed bug, something of the sort. Which is why fumigation of clothing and bedding is so vital."

"Why do other doctors not know these things?"

He smiled grimly. "They have not had my training. The Chinese are far more advanced in their knowledge and treatment of disease than we are. Almost everything I learned as a doctor here I had to throw away when I was trained by my Master Zhanghu-Zi."

She reached up on tip toe and kissed his cheek. "Thank you. I thank God for you every day. Without you Papa would be dead, I'm sure of it."

"Hetty," he cupped her face and kissed her gently. The touch of his lips was a searing delight and a comfort. "And I thank the spirit of heaven for ye every day," he murmured, letting her go with obvious reluctance.

She resisted the urge to dive back into his arms. It was inappropriate and dangerous. *What was she going to do?*

CHAPTER 8

The morning following her father's first day free of fever Hetty sat down to breakfast to find a flat rectangular package by her plate. By the shape of it, it was a book. She looked at it puzzled. Where had that come from?

"Mrs Corcoran?" she asked as the woman bustled in with a tray of breakfast items. "Where did this come from?"

"It was delivered this morning Miss Rooke."

Hetty turned it over while Mrs Corcoran laid out her breakfast, eggs and toast with small bowls of butter and jam and a pot of tea.

She found a small note affixed to the bottom with sealing wax and peeled it off. Opening the folded card, she read the letters T O Y L

There was no signature. She opened the package which was wrapped in tissue paper and tied with a white ribbon. It was a book. A slender volume of Wordsworth's Poems, and she knew at once who had sent it. It was Merlow. He had formed the habit of taking her for a walk when time permitted, and they had spoken of poetry the other day and she admitted to a weakness for Wordsworth.

She hugged the book to her chest and blinked back tears. How like him in the midst of everything to find the time to send her something he thought she would like. *But what did the letters mean?* She would have to ask him when she thanked him for the gift. Really, he was impossible to resist. She had been doing her best to keep him at arms-length and then he did things like this.

She really shouldn't accept gifts from him, it wasn't appropriate when she couldn't accept his proposal, and yet…

She set the book down by her plate and opened to a random page to read while she ate her breakfast.

Having finished her breakfast, she wondered what she could give him as a token of her gratitude. Papa was on the mend, and it was all thanks to him. Principally what he needed was another pair of hands with all the sickness still raging in the village. While papa was mending, others were falling ill. *Perhaps now that papa was getting better, she could help him more?*

She went upstairs to check on her father who was dozing quietly in the sun coming through the window. Seb sat in a chair with a book and cat. She trod over to the window quietly and tugged the curtain across a little to stop the sun hitting her father's face.

Seb looked up and smiled.

She gestured to him to follow her out to the landing. Quietly she said, "If I offer to help Merlow with the other patients can you still keep an eye on Papa? I think he is mending nicely but he still needs watching."

"Aye I can relieve Mrs Corcoran for a few hours each day. George Nieves is coping with the tap just fine for me at the moment."

"Thank you," she smiled and kissed his cheek.

"Is the good doctor keeping the line, Hetty?"

She flushed and straightened, "Of course! What a question, Seb! With sickness in the village, it wouldn't be appropriate, and in any case, I'm not encouraging him."

"Aren't you now? Doesn't look like to me," said her big brother with a look that made her blush even harder.

"I promise you Seb, nothing – nothing untoward is going on, Doctor Thornton is a gentleman."

"Hm. Well it's a good notion for you to help him, the poor man looked exhausted last time I saw him."

She smiled and went off to change her gown for one of her older ones and then she headed down to the surgery to offer her services.

She knocked on the door and waited, wondering if he was even at home. Lately he had often been out all night, like he was with little Benjamin O'Donnell. She swallowed the lump in her throat. That was a tragedy the village was never going to get over.

She knocked again and was just deciding he wasn't at home when the door opened. He was bleary eyed and rumpled, his hair uncombed and his cheeks stubbled above his beard, showing he hadn't shaved and trimmed it for a few days.

His tired eyes lit up at the sight of her. "Hetty love! What is it?" His expression dimmed. "Yer father's not worse?"

"No on the contrary he is better, which has prompted me to ask if you need some help. I can leave Papa with Seb and Mrs Corcoran; he doesn't need to be watched every minute now. I also," she flushed. "Wanted to thank you for my book, that was so sweet of you."

He shook his head. "Ye welcome lass, I know ye've a partiality for the man, and I had a volume in my library, thought I'd make ye a present of it."

"Well thank you." She paused and then asked a little shyly, "what do the letters signify?"

"TOYL? Thinking of you, love," he said with a smile.

She flushed and looked down, unable to meet the warm look in his eyes. *Oh, dear what was she going to do?*

An awkward pause ensued until she finally said with an effort. "Do you need help?"

"Aye, but I'm reluctant to ask ye love, its hard and frequently unpleasant."

"You know me well enough surely by now, that I am not squeamish?"

"I do. I'd love yer help if yer willing. Come in. Patients will start showing up soon, I'll explain how ye can help me best?"

She nodded and followed him into the house.

. . .

85

TWO NIGHTS later Merlow got another one of those late-night call outs he dreaded. Dragged from sleep by a thunderous knock on the front door, he staggered downstairs. He'd taken to sleeping fully clothed, it saved time.

It was Mitch Stewart.

"Doc, you have to come, it's Maggie she taken bad with the fever."

Merlow grabbed his bag, which he kept by the door fully stocked, and shrugged into his jacket.

"Has she a rash?"

"Aye doc, it's the typhus I know it," fretted Mitch. "She complained of feeling tired and sore earlier in the day but thought she'd just over done it with cleaning out the barn the other day, she's a fanatical housewife, I can't stop her cleaning and such like."

Merlow nodded thinking that Maggie had likely picked up a bite while in the barn. He was forced to stride out to keep up with Mitch's long legs, the man was several inches taller and broader than him, and he wasn't a small man himself.

"Just a moment, while I alert Hetty, Miss Rooke. She's nursed her father through this fever and he's mending nicely, she knows what to do and can help you with nursing Maggie." Mitch nodded and paced while Merlow knocked and let Hetty know her services were needed. She nodded and said, "Mitch, I'm so sorry. Just give me a few minutes to dress and I'll be right over. Go on without me, I'll see you soon."

Merlow nodded and he accompanied Mitch to his house on the other side of the bridge. They found Maggie standing swaying in the middle of the sitting room shivering in her night gown. She stared at them glassy eyed and muttered, "must finish the laundry."

"No Maggie love," soothed Mitch, scooping her up and taking her upstairs to their bedchamber, where he got her between the sheets again. She tossed restlessly, plucking at the sheets and muttering things neither of them could understand. "You see what she's like Doc, can you help her?"

"I hope so Mitch. The first thing to do is take her temperature. You may need to put her in a cold bath. Can you prepare one?"

"Aye," said Mitch hopefully, clearly glad of something practical to do.

"Good, you do that."

HETTY ARRIVED to find Mitch had filled a tub with cold water on Merlow's instructions, and Merlow had administered a dose of his medicine to the patient.

"The fever is spiking dangerously high," Merlow said quietly to her in the corridor, having left Mitch to watch his wife and stop her getting out of bed. "You can help Mitch bathe her to get the fever down. You know how to administer the thermometer to measure her temperature?"

"Yes, you showed me," she said steadily.

"Good, Mitch won't want me seeing his wife naked, but he won't mind if you do. Stay with them. I'll come back in an hour. Since I'm up, I'll do a round of my other patients check, that their all right."

She nodded and squeezed his hand before re-entering the bedroom to help Mitch with Maggie.

It was a long night and Maggie's fever remained stubbornly high despite their best efforts. And worse, her lungs were congesting, Hetty could hear it in her laboured breathing. Maggies symptoms were coming on more rapidly than papa's had. Hetty was worried, but tried not to show it in front of Mitch, who was beside himself to see his dear Maggie in such straights.

When Merlow visited them a third time, just before dawn, to administer more of the medicine, she drew him out of the bedchamber to voice her concerns.

"She seems worse than Papa was? I didn't think that could be possible," she said softly.

"Aye lass I know, I think we need to try the menthol steam bowl to clear her lungs I don't like the sound of her breathing."

Hetty nodded and headed downstairs to put the kettle on.

When she returned with steaming bowl of water and a towel, Mitch had Maggie sitting up with pillows. Merlow added the menthol drops to the bowl and Hetty set it on the nursing table over Maggies legs, while Mitch tried to get maggie to bend over the bowl and breathe.

"Come sweeting it'll make you feel better," he pleaded as she fought him, tossing he head and muttering under her breath. A hacking coughing fit assailed her, and Mitch held her still as Hetty dived for the bowl to stop it going everywhere.

When the coughing eased, Mitch tried again and managed to get her head over the bowl under the towel. It eased her breathing a little after a few minutes and Mitch settled her back against the pillows while Hetty took the bowl away.

"Best to keep her propped up with pillows, it should help with the congestion," said Merlow. "Rub some of this on her chest and try the bowl every few hours." He handed Mitch a pot of the menthol emollient. Mitch nodded, his face etched with worry and fatigue. "And remember to try and keep her fluids up," he added.

BUT DESPITE ALL THEIR EFFORTS, forty-eight hours later, Maggie drew her last painful breath. Mitch was stunned. Hetty distraught at her inability to save the woman. She was also out on her feet with exhaustion.

Leaving Mitch to the care of the neighbours who all rallied round to help, Hetty let Merlow take her home.

"Why?" she asked helplessly, wiping tears off her cheeks.

"I don't know lass. Sometimes it happens like this."

"Maggie was a good woman!" said Hetty vehemently.

"I know," Merlow put an arm round her. They were standing in the lee of the vicarage porch; it was barely daylight.

"Was it my fault? Did I do something wrong? Not do enough?"

"No love. Ye did everything ye could. Just sometimes it's not enough and only the Great Spirit knows why."

"Little Benjamin and now Maggie!" Hetty wept. "Poor Mitch!" she said soggily.

"I know, he'll bear watching. I don't think it's sunk in with him yet."

Hetty sniffed and wiped her eyes. "I'd best go in and tell Papa, he will be so upset, especially because he is too frail yet to help."

"Get some sleep yerself, love ye're exhausted!" He admonished her gently.

"I know," she sighed wearily. "But I feel too wound up to sleep."

"Do your best, and don't forget to eat something!" he said as she opened the door.

WHEN MERLOW CALLED to take her out for their daily walk later that afternoon, he was told she was asleep. Sorry to have missed her company, but glad she was sleeping, he left a small bouquet of flowers he had picked for her on the way. Wildflowers grew in profusion on the common and she had admired them the other day. He wished he had time to secure some of her favourite violets, but he had no time to spare for that at the moment.

It wrenched his heart to see her so upset this morning, but he shared her sorrow, for Maggie Stewart was a good woman who would be sadly missed by them all. As a healer he'd lost many patients over the years, but he remember very clearly his first one. It bites the deepest and leaves a scar. Hetty would be feeling that over Maggie.

With a sigh he turned away from the vicarage porch only to be called back by Mrs Corcoran. "Doctor! Miss Hetty left these for you," she said offering him a cloth tied up with a bow. It's some of her biscuits," she added by way of explanation. "She couldn't sleep this morning poor lamb, so she baked instead. She set these aside for you."

He grinned, his heart surging with hope.

"Please thank her for me Mrs Corcoran, " he said taking the bundle.

"I will that Doctor." She waved him off and closed the door. He stood in the street a moment staring up at the window of Hetty's room, cradling the biscuits in his arms. "I love ye sweetheart," he murmured. "I do hope ye'll see yer way clear to loving me back."

He walked slowly back to his house, his head and heart a warm fuzz of love and hope.

But his hopes were dashed the next day when he called to take her out again and she told him she couldn't.

She pale and tired and he was instantly worried.

"You haven't a fever or a rash?" he asked.

She shook her head. "No, I'm just weary. I-" she stopped. "Please Merlow, I'm just not up to it today."

"Of course, love." He kissed her fingers, and she withdrew them with a grimace and stepped back. He stepped back and she shut the door on him.

It's just grief, he told himself *and being physically exhausted*. He tried very hard not to see it as a rejection of himself. But he began to wonder if, despite everything, she didn't, couldn't or wouldn't return his feelings no matter what he did?

CHAPTER 9

*I*t was a full month later before the fever had run its course in the village. The death toll was confined to three. Little Benjamin, old Mr Pierson who refused to leave with the others, and Maggie Stewart. It was still three too many in Merlow's view, but the numbers were remarkably low thanks to the preventative measures and the nursing strategies he and Hetty implemented. The vicar was still frail and tired easily, but he was free of the fever. The curate, Mr Ferson Partridge, was on permanent loan at the moment until Mr Rooke was back to full strength. Everyone who had gone away was back home and life was getting back to normal as much as it could after such a tragedy.

When weather permitted, his evening walks with Hetty had become the highlight of his day, their time to talk and be together in amongst the stress of caring for the villagers. Hetty's calm commonsense and caring manner with the patients made her an invaluable asset, and confirmed in his mind her absolute suitability as a doctor's wife. If he wasn't already in love with her, he'd have offered for her for the sheer practicality of it.

The problem was Hetty was still behaving skittishly. During the intensity of caring for her father she had allowed him to hold and kiss her, but in the aftermath of Maggies passing she became more distant. Barely allowing him to hold her hand or press a kiss to her forehead. It was driving him mad. And if he mentioned marriage she laughed it off or changed the subject. While they were so deeply mired in caring for the sick, he felt it inappropriate to push the point, but village life was returning to some semblance of normality now, and he felt an urgent need to bring Hetty to the point.

For autumn, the weather was being unseasonably warm and dry, and he arrived on her doorstep to collect her for their evening stroll with a blanket and a picnic basket and a plan to get Hetty to let her guard down.

"What's this?" she said closing the front door and eyeing his burdens.

"I thought we could have supper on the riverbank. I know a nice spot where we can enjoy the last of the sun, and I think you deserve a little reward for all your hard work."

"My hard work?" she protested falling into step beside him. "All I've done is help out where I can. It is you who have borne the brunt of it."

"You have shared that burden with me, and I appreciate it," he said firmly.

They strolled down the main street to the bridge where it crossed the river and diverged off the path to walk along the riverbank path until they reached the spot he had in mind. It was secluded and private, and still caught the afternoon sun, so it was warm and dry. The river burbled past over the rocks and birds chirped and bobbed about among the rushes and the trees. It was a perfect little oasis.

"Oh, this is lovely!" she said, sitting down on the blanket he'd laid down and drawing the picnic basket toward her to see what was in it. She unpacked the bottle of wine and glasses, plates, bread, cheese, olives and dates he had brought. It was simple fare but enough, he hoped, to make her feel comfortable and relaxed.

Joining her on the blanket, he uncorked the wine and filled the glasses, finding a flat spot to put them down on, before tackling the bread, cheese, olives and dates and offering her a plate.

"Thank you," she said tucking into the food. "I confess I missed luncheon today; I was so busy sorting out the last details for the church fête, on Saturday."

"You had a committee meeting without me?"

"I knew you were busy." she said taking a bite of bread and cheese and closing her eyes in bliss. Her expression made him think of making her look like that for other reasons, causing him to stifle something half sigh and half groan.

"Besides, confess, you only came to the meetings so that you could talk to me afterwards."

"Miss Rooke, I'll have you know I was perfectly serious about helping with the fête. But yes, I will confess you were the main attraction. You still are." He offered her the glass, which she took, and tilted his to touch hers lightly. "To the most beautiful woman in Pinner."

She blushed and shook her head. "I wish you wouldn't. You know it's not true."

"It is to me," he said quietly, holding her gaze with his. "When can I instruct your father to put up the banns Hetty?"

She looked so flummoxed he almost recanted. But no, he had to push, or she'd keep him on a string forever. He added with gently irony, "But I'm getting ahead of myself, aren't I? You haven't said yes, yet."

"Merlow!" she said helplessly.

At least she hadn't gone back to calling him Doctor Thornton.

He put the glasses aside and took her hands in his. "Hetty, will you tell me what makes you hesitate? I'm not repugnant to you, am I?"

"No of course not," she said with visible distress.

"And you might even like me a little?" he said with a hopeful smile.

"I like you a lot! You know that." She said with a sad expression that wrung his heart.

"Then what is it sweetheart?" he probed gently. He was almost certain he knew the reason, but he needed her to trust him enough to tell him.

"I- I cannot!" He could see the tears start to her eyes as she looked away, blinking and his heart squeezed painfully in his chest. His instinct was to stop pushing her, it hurt her so. But he also knew that if he couldn't establish trust between them, it would undermine their marriage, and he didn't mean for it to begin with secrets between them. He had several of his own and he'd confess them in time too.

Was it unfair of him to expect her to go first? Perhaps, but hers was a much more forgivable one than his. He needed to be sure of her feelings for him before he confessed to manslaughter.

Which was selfish, but he wanted Hetty more than he'd ever wanted anything in his life, and he recognised that he wasn't prepared to be entirely fair if it increased the odds of losing her.

Deciding on a change of tack, he drew her into his arms and settled them down onto the blanket. She didn't fight him, which was good. She nestled her head into his shoulder and sighed. He ran a hand up and down her side in soothing fashion, letting things settle between them into a companionable silence.

"It doesn't matter Hetty," he said softly against her hair. "I know you think it does, but it doesn't. I love you, nothing you can tell me will change that."

Her hand clutched the lapel of his jacket at his words, and he waited in silence. *Would it be enough to encourage her confession?* But she remained stubbornly silent. Suppressing a sigh of frustration, he stroked her hair and pushed her chin up so that he could see her face. She smiled at him tearfully, and he almost gave up. He couldn't keep doing this to her.

Cupping her face, he kissed her, a soft tender kiss, deepening to something more. He'd kept all their kisses since her father got ill from developing into anything passionate, it had seemed inappropriate. But now, passion was perhaps the weapon of last resort in his fight to win her heart. And his

Taoist training in the arts of love would stand him in good stead here, for its emphasis on the heightening of female pleasure and restraint of male release would give him the discipline required, he hoped, to make her feel safe and lower her guard.

Pressing her slowly back into the blanket he kissed her with devastating thoroughness, and she didn't resist, more, she responded, tentatively at first and then with growing enthusiasm that lifted his heart with hope, as it fired his blood with heat and aching pleasure. She was exquisite and he wanted her desperately. But his own needs were irrelevant in this moment.

He slid his hand slowly up her side, his thumb caressing her abdomen with little circles as he went. Feeling the heat of her body through the fabric of her gown, while his lips and tongue plundered her mouth. She made little noises in her throat which gave him thrills. His hand reached the underside of her breast, and he cupped it gently, giving the lovely, soft handful a light squeeze. His thumb scraped across her nipple feeling it perk up under his touch, he stifled a groan and pressed his groin into the blanket to staunch the flood of heat that provoked in him. *Training! Discipline!* He reminded himself.

She gasped and stiffened under his touch, and he wondered if he'd gone too fast for her. She fought him off and sat up. He propped himself on his elbows looking at her back, her shoulders hunched, her head forward and low.

"Hetty," he said softly.

"I mustn't, it's wrong." Her voice was husky, distressed.

He sat up and pulled her back against him, wrapping his arms round her, he wanted to hug the distress out of her. Love the hurt out of her. *If he ever found out who did this to her...*

"It's not wrong love," he said, his face resting on her hair, she smelled of honeysuckle today. "It's not wrong to want to make you feel good. It's not wrong because I love you, and I've already said I'll marry you tomorrow if you'll let me. I won't do anything to hurt you, I promise." His conscience twinged a bit at that, he was causing her distress now. But he would never hurt her in the way she had been hurt before. She had to let him prove that. "I won't ruin you Hetty, is that what you're afraid of?" he asked the question gently.

She gasped and jerked in his hold. He tightened his arms round her and said softly, "It's alright, sweetheart. I've enough experience and enough self-control not to let things go further than they should." He kissed her hair and the side of her face. He tickled her earlobe delicately with his tongue, which provoked a giggle.

"Merlow!" It was a soft protest, more encouragement than resistance. He laughed gently with her, and she turned in his embrace to look up at him. "I don't deserve this," she said.

"You do," he said emphatically and kissed her again, because he couldn't resist. This was going to be a slow process, but he had all the patience in the world for her. She leaned into the kiss, her hands creeping up round his neck and he let himself sink into the pleasure of her mouth, encouraged by her response.

He eased her down to the blanket again. The

sun was casting long shadows across the water and the grass now, but its rays were still warm on his back as he pressed her to the blanket, one hand resting lightly on her hip, while he deepened the kiss.

Kissing along her jaw and neck and back to her mouth, he let his thumb rub gently into the hollow of her hip-bone and felt the ripple of her response to that lightest and most subtle of touches. The contraction of her muscles that told him of the tingling heat building between her thighs, she was no more immune to the searing fire between them than he was. It was a victory of sorts.

He ran his hand slowly up her side again, resting below her breast, letting his thumb roam and trace circles very gently over her abdomen and then slowly up onto the curve of her breast. His fingers dragged across that nipple again, making it perk up further and provoking a whimpering moan from Hetty as his teeth grazed down the side of her neck, and he pressed a kiss to the soft skin of her throat, murmuring, "feels good doesn't it, love?"

She moved her legs restlessly, and he couldn't suppress a smile. He knew what that meant. She made a noise of agreement, and he found her mouth again to give her more kisses, while his fingertips teased her nipple, with slow gentle strokes over the pert bud, through the fabric of her gown.

His own body burned with an ache he ruthlessly suppressed, despite that, his pulse surged, and his breathing became ragged. His base urge to ravish her, he must control, or all the progress he had made would be lost. He would frighten her and send her fleeing from him if he gave into what he wanted.

Instead, he continued his slow indirect method of arousing her, with touches that set her afire, his aim to push her to a point where she was desperate enough to welcome more intimate strokes. And it was working, he could feel it in the subtle shifting and tightening of her body, in her racing pulse and desperate breaths. The little noises she made, the squirm of her hips and the restless movements of her legs. Her thighs rubbing together. Her hands clutching at him, her lips and tongue desperate for more kisses. The arching of her back and stretching of her neck.

He squeezed her lovely breast gently and then moved his hand to rest on her solar plexus, feeling the rapid beat of her pulse and the rise and fall of her chest as she breathed. Breaking the kiss and propping his head on his other hand he gazed down at her face, noting the redness of her chin from the prickles of his beard, her swollen lips and wide, darkened eyes in the fading light. "Alright love?" he asked, his voice husky.

She blinked up at him, visibly coming back to herself. But the haze of arousal still sat in the back of her eyes. She licked her lip and let out a breath slowly. She had to trust that he would stop and not take her further than she wanted to go. So as much as he wanted to continue, he paused to let her gather herself.

"Yes," she said at last, her voice soft and low. The note drove straight to his groin, and he had to fight against showing a visceral reaction, even as unbearable heat bloomed behind his breeches. He drew in a breath and let it out slowly and silently.

That was enough, today, even he couldn't bear it.

"We're going to lose the light soon; I should take you home."

They packed up, and he escorted her to her door where he gave her a lingering kiss goodnight on the porch. And be damned to who ever saw them. The whole village knew he was courting her in any case.

CHAPTER 10

*M*ing was impatient to be off, but the Englishman wouldn't be hurried, taking the time to wash, shave and eat breakfast.

"The name is Durand Percival, by the way," he said sipping his tea and cutting into the thick slices of salted pork on his plate. Which had been fried along with the eggs. Ming, who was an abstemious eater shuddered and made do with the bread and cheese on offer. Food in this country was abominable and extremely unhealthy.

"Ming Liang," he responded, sipping his own tea. "Family name Ming," he added for clarification. Because the ignorant Englishman, would assume the reverse.

Percival held out his hand with a smile. "Nice to meet you."

Ming looked at the hand a moment and then shook it. He knew enough of foreign customs to recognise a gesture of friendliness when he saw it.

"Do you have a horse?" asked Percival, mopping up egg with a slice of bread.

"No."

"Well, that is the first thing we need to sort out. Do you have any money."

"Yes."

"Good. Would you like me to negotiate a deal for you?"

Ming inclined his head graciously. The Englishman might irritate him, but he was trying to be friendly and useful. "Thank you."

After breakfast Percival secured him a mount, "at a good price," he assured him, and they were able to get underway. It was a drizzly, cloudy day with a bit of wind and they both hunkered down in their coats and hats against the weather. Percival was inclined to want to chat, which Ming discouraged with monosyllabic replies, and eventually he gave up, and they rode in blessed silence.

Which left Ming in peace to worry about his men. Cheung's death had shaken him to the core. And what he had to tell him in those dying few moments had shocked him greatly. The Scotsman had proven far more adept at fighting than expected. He had overcome the three of them. Three men against one! It seemed incredible that three highly trained fighters could not best one foreign devil. With defeat staring them in the face, Cheung had fled to bring him word, but his wound had festered, he had lost much blood and only his training had allowed him to continue on back to Scotland and Dysart to try to reach Ming with the news. Cheung had assumed that Ding and Zhou had already perished as the hands of the Scotsman. What he had been able to tell him, however, was where the confrontation had taken place, just outside a place called Oxford. He had not told the Englishman this yet. He had chosen to travel with him for the convenience of having a native speaker and one who was familiar with the culture and habits of the locals, it would make things easier. He had left Cheung's funeral pyre to burn itself out overnight, with an offering and prayers for his freed spirit.

He held out some hope that Ding and Zhou yet lived. They would head to this Oxford and look for them. And then he would find the doctor and exact vengeance for Cheung's death and take possession of the sacred text and the sword that had dealt Cheung's death blow. He fretted for some little while over Ding and Zhou. If they were alive, why had they not returned with the text triumphant? The answer was obvious and not one he wanted to entertain.

Finding this a dead end, his thoughts turned to Aihan. His little sister. *Should he have left her on the Shaolin with a hostile crew? Was their terror of him sufficient to keep her safe?* There was Caishen of course, the boy was faithful and a formidable fighter. He had given his word to protect Aihan with his life. The two were like siblings, having been raised together and more like his children, due to the age difference.

Not that Aihan couldn't take care of herself in a fight. He had trained her well and she was a fierce little warrior. But she was slender, and light boned and ultimately female. *Was she strong enough to defeat a pack of males if they chose to target her?* She was cunning and smart, that would give her an advantage over dumb sailors, and the Captain would surely keep his men under control. He sighed, moving restlessly in the saddle.

He must trust to the Spirits to keep her safe and to her own wisdom and strength coupled with Caishen's. But with each step that took him away from her, he was conscious of a tug in his chest. Yet he was itchy to reach his goal and take possession of the precious Neidan. To be so close to his life's purpose, drove him forward with renewed determination.

THEY REACHED the outskirts of Oxford, after three weeks on the road, and by then Ming was thoroughly sick of the cheerful Englishman. His desire to get his hands on the Scotsman and the precious Neidan was even stronger, and his patience wearing thin. It took all his considerable training to keep his temper even, and not show the emotions that were tearing him apart underneath.

"Somewhere around here." He said bringing his horse to a stop and dismounting. "We search."

The Englishman dismounted without complaint but asked, "what exactly are we looking for?"

"Signs of a fight. Cheung told me that he, Ding and Zhou confronted the Scotsman somewhere around here. We look until we find something."

"And if there is nothing to find?"

Ming ignored that; his gut was telling him there would be something to find. He was dreading what it would be. "Search," he snapped.

"All right, keep your shirt on," said the other

man, beginning to scan the right side of the road. Ming took the left and they searched the next several miles slowly on foot leading their horses.

It was late afternoon when he spotted something that made his blood run cold. A glimpse of blue quilted fabric poking through a layer of mulch and dirt by the side of the road. He stopped, dropping to his knees, and began scrabbling at the dirt. As he worked a leg clad in the fabric began to emerge. He swore in his own language and continued to uncover his grisly find. His voice must have alerted the other man because he came running.

"What is it?" he asked squatting down beside Ming, narrowly avoiding getting dirt in his face from Ming's frantic digging. As Ming worked, more blue fabric appeared in the dirt. The Englishman rose, stepping back in shock. "My God!"

Ming continued his grim task as his hands uncovered first one, then two Chinese warriors. Ding and Zhou. They had been covered quite shallowly by dirt and mulch in the ditch.

The Englishman staggered away, and the sounds of retching came to Ming's ears. He ignored the other man's distress. When the Englishman could command his stomach, he used his flask to rinse his mouth and returned to Ming's side, keeping his eyes away from the grisly sight.

"What happened do you suppose?"

Ming has spent several minutes inspecting the bodies and several things pointed to his men's use of the preserving elixir. The rictus in their expressions, the fact that their bodies had not commenced to rot, nor been attacked by beasts, despite being only shallowly covered. And finally, despite the blood from some superficial scratches, the apparent absence of fatal wounds on their bodies.

Ming stared at his men with tear-soaked eyes, his expression grim. "I believe they took their own lives. Which means only one thing. They failed in their mission." He swallowed and wiped his face with his sleeve. "The elixir has preserved their bodies; we must now burn the fleshly vessels to ensure their continued journey to the afterlife. The flames will set them free."

DURAND SHOOK his head over this, but three weeks in the General's company meant he knew better than to argue. He had never encountered a more stubborn man in his life. The General's will was implacable.

Breaking through the underbrush on the side of the road they found an open space suitable upon which to build a pyre and began collecting wood for that purpose. When they had a sufficiently dense bed of wood upon which to lay the bodies, came the horrific task of moving them into place from the hollow ditch.

Suppressing the gag reflex with difficulty, Durand heroically lifted the feet of the first corpse, convinced they would come off in his hands. But the body was indeed still well-preserved and nothing so horrendous happened. When they had arranged all three upon the bed, they began to cover them with more branches and piles of leaves. The dry weather meant there was a lot of tinder available.

When the task was complete, Ming knelt and uttered prayers in his own language, made an offering of his meagre rations, and then, using the flint that he carried in his pack, he set multiple sparks that would set the tinder alight from different parts of the pyre.

When these were well lit, he sat cross-legged, closed his eyes and began chanting quietly. Durand, with nothing to do, found a dry spot under a tree away from the direction of the smoke and using his valise as a pillow, took a nap.

It was dark when Ming woke him. The smell of acrid smoke was still heavy in the air, and he could see the glow from the coals and the curls of smoke still rising from the pyre in the dark. He sat up, blinking his eyes which felt gritty, his nose and throat felt raw from the smoke and no doubt his clothing stank of it. He reached for his flask to slake his dry throat.

"All done?" he asked waving at the pyre in gloom.

"Ding and Zhou are free; we can leave them now. The remains of the fire will burn itself out in a few hours. I suggest we move from here and find somewhere to sleep."

"No argument from me," said Durand rising and picking up his valise. They returned to where they had tethered the horses, up wind of the fire. Mounting they headed towards Oxford, where they secured a room for the night at the Crown Inn, the Oxford coaching Inn, in Cornmarket St on the main road through Oxford.

The Crown was a large bustling Inn, busy with patrons but more importantly in Durand's view, a likely good bet for a solid meal and a comfortable bed. His surmise proved correct, and he decided his dwindling resources would stretch to a bath. Not much could be done with the pickled state of his clothing except to air the garments out, which he did by hanging them out the window.

They agreed that they would decide in the morning what to do next. Even Ming's inexhaustible supply of energy seemed drained by the events of the day.

As they had tracked the doctor to this locale courtesy of Ming's man picking up the doctor's trail again from this point would likely prove problematic. Durand certainly hoped they would run the man to earth soon, or he was going to run out of funds. He had not expected to be on the road this long.

After three weeks he was accustomed to Ming's peculiar habits, such as his refusal to sleep in a bed, rolling himself instead into his bed-roll and sleeping on the floor. Waking before dawn and spending an hour sitting cross-legged with his eyes closed, followed by another hour performing peculiar movements involving contortionistic arrangements of his limbs, often in rapid succession with leaps and lunges and chopping motions of the hands. He repeated this routine at night in reverse. He also ate sparingly and was not given to idle chatter. In the course of their sojourn, Durand had learned nothing of what the General wanted with Thornton, or how he and the men they had followed had come to be in Scotland. His attempts to find out had been greeted with silence, and if he persisted, tersely worded threats.

. . .

MING WRAPPED himself in his bedroll, giving the talkative Englishman his back. His soul was sick and tired after today's work, the Scotsman was either a devil or one who was mightily blessed by the Great Spirit, and he didn't know which it was. In either case the man would pay for what he had done.

THE NEXT MORNING, Durand questioned the landlady Mrs Sarah Wakelin over breakfast with no real hope of finding any clue as to the doctor's whereabouts.

"A Scottish gentleman, quite a broad accent, tall with dark brown hair and beard. He would have come through here about two months ago."

"Would he be a doctor, by any chance?" asked Mrs Wakelin.

"Yes!" Durand's pulse quickened. *It couldn't be that easy, could it?*

"Of course, I remember him! He was with Mitch and Maggie Stewart from Pinner, my sister lives there you know. He is going to be their new doctor by all accounts…" she kept talking, but Durand lost focus on her words as the name of Pinner buzzed in his head. Visions of Henrietta Rooke conjured by the mere name of the place. At one point he'd been obsessed with her, but his youthful infatuation proved more lust than love with hindsight. The memories came flooding back, and he flushed with shame, he'd been an ignorant lout back then.

He jerked back to the present as Mrs Wakelin said, "would you like more coffee sir?"

"No, thank you. Mrs Wakelin you have been most helpful," he reached into his pocket and gave her a douceur for her trouble. She took the gold coin with a smile and pocketed it.

CHAPTER 11

When Merlow came for her the next evening, Hetty was quivering with uncertainty and anticipation. She couldn't deny that his kisses and his touch aroused her, made her want to do wanton things. Things she knew she shouldn't. It had kept her awake last night with a restless ache. She had to tell him the truth, but every time she pushed herself to the sticking point, the words locked in her throat. She was so afraid, that despite what he said, if he knew the truth he would turn from her in disgust, and the longer it went on the worse it would be.

He made her feel so loved and cared for, so wrapped up in a warm blanket of care, she desperately wanted to hang onto it for a little bit longer, as much as she felt she didn't deserve it. She ached to tell him she loved him too. But she hung onto the words because the moment she uttered them, she would have no recourse but to agree to their marriage, and then she would have to tell him why she couldn't marry him, or rather watch his love dissolve in front of her eyes and she couldn't bear it. *She was so weak!*

She would tell him tonight, she must!

There were a few clouds about today, a bit of a breeze, so she donned a cloak for warmth and took his arm as he said, "I thought we could take a walk in the spinney today, so if it rains, we will be under shelter?"

"Yes, it does look like we might get a shower or two, the gardens certainly need it, it has been very dry so far this season."

"So, what did you accomplish today?" he asked as they crossed the street and headed for the common that bordered the stand of tree's referred to locally as the spinney.

"I baked this morning, cakes and biscuits for the parishioners. I helped Papa with his sermon preparation for Sunday, he will be doing the first service this week since he became ill. Mr Pierson will assist him. And this afternoon I did my rounds, delivering the goodies I baked this morning. And you?"

"A dozen patients in the clinic and a dozen more house calls. Mitch Stewart is struggling since Maggie's passing, which is natural, but I'm keeping an eye on him."

She nodded, Maggie's loss was still being felt by all of them. "The O'Donnell's too, are suffering. Seb tells me Mr O'Donnell has been at the Bull's Head more than he was used to be."

"Aye. Mitch is struggling to get out of bed. I've seen men with the melancholy before. It takes them in different ways. Some rage, some drink, some just stop. Mitch seems to be one of those." He paused and added quietly, "My father was a rager and a drinker, my brother Col just stopped, by all accounts. I wasna there to see it, but his boys ran wild for several months having to care for themselves when he wouldna get out of bed or the whiskey bottle. He's better now, but the boys suffered. Mitch doesna have children and maybe that's worse for there's no one to drag him out of it."

They had reached the cover of the spinney, a stand of sturdy oaks, a path wandered through them towards the bank of the river that wound in this direction. The thick canopy of huge trees made it darker and more cosy within. Leaf mulch made the floor springy under foot and the leaves on the trees were beginning to turn, but not fall in great numbers yet, the weather had been too mild.

He slipped an arm round her waist beneath her cloak as they walked, and she leaned into him, too weak to resist the pull of his attraction. He stopped beneath the spreading branches of a huge old oak and turned her to face him. "I've missed you Hetty," he said softly and kissed her. She slid her arms up round his neck, and surrendered to his kiss, pulled tight against his body, she gave into the clamour in her own for his touch.

Emboldened by yesterday, she angled her head for a better, deeper, kiss and sank into the pure delight of his mouth on hers. His hands ran over her back, under her cloak, and pressed her closer against him, she couldn't miss the heat and hardness in his breeches and knew she should pull back, should be alarmed by what that meant, but her old fears seemed to be dissipating. It was different with Merlow, instinctively she knew that.

The latent desire he'd stirred in her body yesterday leapt to life again in a fiery flood, making her press closer, kiss harder, clutch tighter.

He walked her backwards a few steps until her back connected with the trunk of the tree, his mouth traced kisses down her neck, and she arched it to let him, pressing her breasts against his chest, they felt heavy and ached for more of the attention they had received yesterday.

There was a small part of her brain that was telling her this was unwise, and she should stop, make him stop; but paradoxically, because she knew he would stop if she asked, she didn't want to ask.

His hands came up to clasp each breast and massage them and the relief made her moan in delight. His fingers found her nipples and scraped over them as he had done yesterday with a single breast, this time he did it with both and the effect was electric, sending arrows of heat and tingling pleasure to the place between her legs.

Her nipples were tight, aching buds, as his fingers caressed them, pinching lightly through the fabric of her gown.

He abandoned one breast to run a hand down her belly and press lightly between her thighs, precisely at that point that burned and throbbed. The bolt of pleasure that light pressure provoked even through her petticoats, made her moan aloud, her hips tilting instinctively to press into his touch.

He broke the kiss to rest his forehead against hers and say husky voiced. "Is this alright, love?"

She gasped blinking at him and he pressed again.

"May I touch you?" He asked, an aching note in his voice that pulled at her, turning her limbs liquid with desire.

She nodded, entirely unable to find her voice.

He wrapped an arm round her and kissed her deeply, while his free hand lifted her skirts, until he could reach under them and run a hand lightly up her thighs. His fingers quested higher until they reached that point of burning heat and the merest touch of one fingertip made her whole-body jerk, and provoked a groan from them both.

"Hetty, love your so wet!" he murmured in delight.

She gasped as his finger parted the soft folds of her sex and stroked ever so gently. The pleasure was so sharp it was almost painful. He tightened his arm round her as her legs threatened to buckle, and she clung to him, whimpering.

"It's alright, I've got you," he soothed. His finger traced up and down, mesmerizingly slowly, the heat and tingling pleasure radiating outwards from his touch sending her pulse and breathing wild and stoking the fire between her legs higher and higher.

It was the most blissful feeling she had every experienced and not enough at the same time. He kissed her slow and deep as he stroked, sliding up and down gently, at the top of the stroke his finger grazed something that made her almost jump out of her skin with sensation, it was so sharp it made her cry out and cling to him.

He broke the kiss to watch her face as he did it

again, very, very lightly and then swirled his finger in a circle round that spot, which made her knees give out, as tingling heat bloomed and took her breath away.

"Merlow!" she gasped.

"I know love," he whispered hoarsely.

"Please." She didn't even know what she was asking for exactly, just something to relieve the ache, the burning pleasure.

"Yes, my darling," his voice had dropped to a gravelly ache, that thrummed through her body as if she were a harp and his fingers conducted the note in his voice deep into her body. She felt incandescent, as her back arched, pressing closer to his touch, wanting more and more, as his fingers slowly increased in speed.

Until the pleasure built to breaking point, and she burst in a hot cloud of bliss that stopped her breath and left her in a state of endless nerve tingling pleasure for a moment outside of time. Her body trembled with it and the cascading delight pulsed downwards like the wavelets breaking outwards from a dropped pebble. Until she hung limp and gasping in his embrace, her heart thudding hard and heavy in her breast, the throbbing, swollen flesh between her legs, a tympani in time with her heart.

His fingers stilled, and he withdrew his hand from beneath her skirts letting them fall round her ankles as he cradled her close against him, holding her weight with his arms and tracing soft kisses over her face and hair and murmuring words in Gaelic she didn't understand.

Feeling drugged, she nuzzled her face into his coat and said muzzily, "what was that?"

"Mo luaidh, tha thu bòidheach, tha gaol agam ort" he repeated. "It means, my darling, ye are beautiful, I love ye."

"Oh," she swallowed, her throat closing over with tears. She must tell him now. She must.

Just then an almighty crack of thunder and lightning followed by the roar of rain pelting on the canopy above their heads, made her squeak with fright.

"That was close," he said above the roar of the rain. "Come we had best run; another strike could find this tree and fry us in the bargain."

"Is it not safe under the trees?"

"Not with lightening about. A tree can conduct the strike into the ground and catch us in the process. Come," he wrapped an arm round her, and they fled back along the path and out onto the common. They were soaked to the skin in moments, the rain was so heavy; and the clouds so dark, almost all the light had gone. They made their way back to the street and to the vicarage.

"Do you want to come in?" she said, breathless from their headlong flight.

He shook his head.

"Best if I head straight home and change. Make sure ye change immediately I don't want ye catching a cold." he kissed her quickly and left. She let herself into the house and headed straight upstairs to remove her soaked garments and dry her hair.

Sitting by the fire combing out her hair, her thoughts inevitably strayed to what had happened beneath the trees. She had washed herself after she stripped and found a lot of sticky fluid between her legs. Her flesh was still tender and swollen. The aftermath so similar and yet completely different from what she had experienced before.

For one thing, she had never known a woman could experience that incandescent explosion of pleasure. She had thought only men experienced that. If it was like that for men too, and she must assume it was, it was no wonder they sought it out and took it from women whenever they could. It was also no wonder that so many women and girls were lured into surrendering their virtue for such a prize. Yet she had not been gifted with that prize when she was a girl. Nothing but pain and blood and shame.

She shuddered, her thoughts shying from those memories that she had kept buried deep and tried not to think of for so many years. Since Merlow's advent, she had struggled to keep those memories at bay. She could no longer pretend to herself that she didn't *wish* to be married, to be loved, to have a family of her own. Not when the man of her dreams was determined to marry her. Determined to bury her in an avalanche of love and care, and God forgive her, pleasure...

She almost groaned aloud recalling what he had done to her tonight. *What would have happened next if the storm hadn't hit? Would he have pushed for his own pleasure?* His behaviour was so different from what she had experienced before she didn't know what to think.

What would have happened is that she would

have blurted out the truth, because she could no longer keep it inside.

And after tonight she had to face the reality that she could no longer continue to hide the truth from him. She had to be brave enough to face the consequences of her past. *She would make a full confession tomorrow, after the fête was over.*

MERLOW STRIPPED off his soaked clothing and towelled himself dry, well pleased with his ability to bring Hetty pleasure, but irritated by the storm's interruption of their intimacy. *Had she been about to share her secret in the aftermath?* He would likely never know.

He could only hope that he had established a foundation for her trust. That she would finally share the truth with him, because he recognised that until she did, she would not consent to marry him. Perhaps he had to confront her with it, make it clear he knew and understood, did not blame her and would not hold it against her. The trouble was he didn't know the specifics. He had all but told her he didn't care that she wasn't a virgin, but she seemed not to understand what he was saying. What he had learned to tonight was that he was the first to bring her pleasure.

Wanting her was driving him crazy, but it would be worth it in the end he was sure of it. He collapsed naked into the chair by the fire and closed his eyes, overcome by a mixture of fatigue and itchy, unslaked desire. Kissing her, touching her, rousing her, making her come, his body was a battleground of aching need. Despite his training it was impossible to suppress the clamour for release. He could try to meditate it away, but frankly he didn't want to. Giving into the inevitable he got up and found the little pot of unguent he kept for the purpose in his bedside table drawer, he smeared some on his palm and lying down on the bed he took himself in hand.

With slow strokes he relived every delicious moment of Hetty's kisses, her response to his touch and her spectacular release. His imagination took him from there to other firsts. From kisses and touches and squeezes, licks, suckles and strokes, to plunging fingers and finally his cock buried deep inside her.

With a deep groan his body gave up its seed in a heated burst of pleasure on his belly and he lay panting, as the tingles subsided, and pleasures aftermath left him limp and drowsy. He was exhausted with his daily routine of meditation and physical training, work and worry and the discipline he'd imposed upon himself to win Hetty's trust. To win her love. He ached for the moment she would admit the way she really felt. *What if he was wrong, and she didn't love him in return? That she was incapable of it because of the hurts from her past? The longer she held out against him, the more likely this seemed to be the case. What would he do then?* The thought chilled him, and he rolled onto his side pulling up the covers to warm his suddenly cold flesh.

CHAPTER 12

$\mathcal{T}$he day of the Church fête dawned bright, clear and sunny. Hetty was up at dawn to begin her baking and once all her cakes, slices and biscuits were done, she removed her floury apron and went to the Church hall to begin setting up the trestle tables and chairs for the cake and craft stalls, where anyone donating items to the fête for fund-raising, could display their wares.

She found Mrs Craig and Mr Beatson there before her, and as she turned around to fetch the tablecloths from the linen cupboard, she saw the good doctor entering with the plan for the stalls and booths that would occupy the lawn between the hall and the Church.

Everyone with something to sell had a stall, and a portion of their takings would go towards the Church fund. The remaining booths were turned over to entertainment. A Punch and Judy show, a huge barrel for apple bobbing, quoits and pin-the-tail-on-the-donkey.

In addition to these, there was a space for the

village band to set up, they would provide the music for dancing later on. And in the field behind the Church, an archery butt was being set up and an arena for caber tossing and wood chopping.

Seb and Beth had a stall to provide food and drink, to be flanked by the bakery on one side and Mr Beatson's prize cow Bessie, to provide fresh milk, on the other. His daughter was doing to milking. It was on account of Bessie that the doctor had come into the hall.

"Beatson," he said hailing the farmer. "Bessie's no behavin' can ye come give yer lassie a hand wi her?"

"Oh aye," said Beatson pushing a chair into place behind a trestle. " She's usually quite placid, what ails her?"

"Pierson's dog yapped and spooked her, just as Gail was gettin' her settled."

"Ah. She's always been a bit chary of dogs since she was a calf. One of the cattle dogs gave her fright and she's never recovered. I'll come settle her," he said heading for door.

The doctor smiled at Hetty and approached her. "Everythin' under control lass?"

"Yes, thank you," she said trying to pretend that seeing him didn't give her a rush of pleasure. She could feel her cheeks going pink in spite of herself, recalling their last encounter beneath the trees in the storm.

"Weel I'd best get on," he said with obvious reluctance. "Most of the stallholders have claimed their spots. Yer brother is already dispensing pots of ale to the workers. I'll speak with ye later lass, but if ye need anything, ye know where t' find me."

She nodded watching him walk away. The fête wouldn't open officially until eleven, but that wouldn't stop the stallholders buying things off each other before the crowds piled in. She was hopeful of a good turn out from Harrow given how fine the weather was.

Mrs Craig helped her dress the tables with their cloths and then collect her baking items from the rectory kitchen, where she found her father inspecting the goods.

"Hetty!" he exclaimed at sight of her. "Gosh my dear, you have been busy! They smell divine. Good morning, Mrs Craig, I trust you are well?"

"I am vicar," she said with a smile. "And that you are fully recovered?"

"I am. I am. Fit as a fiddle!"

Hetty begged to differ, but didn't say so. The illness had taken its toll on him, and its effects were still to be seen in his thinner than usual frame, and the way he tired more easily than he used to. That was another consideration that weighed on her, when contemplating Merlow's proposal. *Even if he should still wish to marry her when she told him her awful secret, should she leave Papa?*

The vicar helped them take the baked goods out to the hall and arrange them on one of the trestle tables. The Misses Fielding were setting up their craft stall with all the pieces of embroidery and knitting they had made over the preceding year for this occasion. Socks and scarves, slippers and pillows, handkerchiefs and dolls. The vicar stopped to talk to them and admire their work before moving onto Mrs Corcoran's jam and pudding table.

· · ·

AT HALF PAST TEN, Hetty slipped away to go and change into her best day gown for the occasion, pinning her hair into a becoming style on top her head with a fall of curls about her shoulders. It was less severe than her usual practical chignon, and she hoped that Merlow would like it. And she also hoped that she wouldn't scandalise the village by having her hair down.

Running back downstairs, she exited the back door of the vicarage and crossed the garden to the Church and through it to the side entrance from the vestry, that gave onto the open lawn between it and the hall. It was now crowded with stalls arranged in a horseshoe shape and beginning to fill up with customers. Many she recognised, but increasingly she saw strangers and was excited by the prospect that this might be their most successful fête ever.

Edging through a break between booths into the courtyard space in the middle, she was brought up short by the sight of the doctor, who had also obviously gone home to change. *He was wearing a kilt, and my lord didn't he look good in it!* She had never seen him in a kilt before. He wore a jacket with it, over his shirt and waistcoat and the combination was quite devastating. He was talking to Seb, but he must have sensed her staring at him because he turned his head and smiled at her. She walked towards them, drawn to his side like a lodestone.

"A kilt, Doctor Thornton," she said. "Is this your tartan?"

"Aye, lass," he waved at the fabric in blue and green squares with red, yellow and white crossed stripes. "I thought I'd best dress for the occasion, ye ken?"

If she were alone with him, she'd tell him how handsome he looked, but she wasn't going to say so in front of her brother.

"The numbers are looking promising Het," said Seb with a nod to the building crowd.

"Yes, seems like all our hard work might pay off."

SOME HOURS later she concluded the fête was a resounding success. All her baked goods were sold, and she was able to leave her table and circulate round the booths and venture over to the archery butt and caber tossing field, where she found Merlow down to his shirt sleeves tossing cabers with O'Donnell and his son Matt.

Cabers in three sizes were provided for different size and weight competitors as the bigger and stronger the tosser, the more advantage they had. Seb and Mitch Stewart, were the biggest men in the village and would play off after this, the middleweight division.

As caber tossing was a national sport in Scotland, she rather thought Merlow might have an advantage, and she silently willed him to win. She watched tensely as Seb and Mitch steadied the caber for him until he was able to rest it on his shoulder and get his clasped hands under the end of the long pole of larch wood. He ran a few paces forward and lifted the caber. It flew up into the air and flipped end over end to land away from him and fall at 11.00 o'clock. Which was close to a near perfect score. The ideal was for it to land at 12.00 o'clock away from the tosser.

Mr O'Donnell was next, and his caber landed at 3.00 o'clock. Then Matt had ago. His was better than his father's, landing at 9.00 o'clock. Merlow was declared the winner of his division and congratulated by all the men. Seb gave him a tankard of beer and got ready for his own battle with Mitch.

"Seb will win this," said a voice beside Hetty, and she turned to see her sister-in-law Beth, standing beside her, watching Seb with devoted eyes.

"I expect so," said Hetty. "Mr Stewart doesn't look too steady on his feet."

Merlow and O'Donnell steadied the bigger caber for Seb, and when Seb had it securely, he lumbered forward a few steps and launched the Caber into the air. It went higher than Merlow's toss, and spun end over end neatly, before landing and falling at 10 o'clock.

Mitch Stewart stepped up, and again Merlow and O'Donnell helped him steady the caber. Mitch lurched forward and tossed, but the caber failed to flip and landed awkwardly falling back towards Mitch. Which made Seb the clear winner. Mitch shrugged his shoulders and staggered off to the side, picking up his flagon on the way. Hetty watched him go with a concerned frown. *What had Merlow said about Mr Stewart last night? That he was struggling with melancholy over Maggie's death. He'd taken it hard and wasn't coping, that was obvious.*

At least he had put in an appearance today, but it seemed like he was taking solace from his tankard. She swung her gaze back to Merlow, and caught him watching Mitch too with a concerned frown.

The lightweight team, with the smallest and lightest cabers, had already tossed and young Leery Carson was the winner of that bout.

Merlow was the technical overall winner, as his caber had landed in the highest scoring position, so he won two ribbons for his efforts and the congratulations of the men.

Hetty approached him after the men had dissipated.

"I think you had an advantage," she said teasingly.

"Ye think?"

"How often have you tossed a caber?"

He shrugged. "A few times."

She took his arm as they strolled across the field towards the archery butt. The women's competition was in full flight.

"Ye should have a go at this," he said.

She shook her head. "I couldn't hit a barn door at twenty paces." She tightened her grip on his arm and looked up at him. "Is Mitch alright?"

"No, I don't think so. I'll have t' keep an eye on him."

"Mr O'Donnell seems slightly better today," she said.

"Aye, he has good days and bad, Mitch's seem mostly bad."

"What can you do for him?"

"There's a tincture I can give him, if he'll take it mind."

"Of?"

"St John's Wort. It's good for melancholy."

She nodded, "I think I've heard of that." She glanced at the sky to gauge the time. "The bonfire will be lit soon, and supper served, I'd best be getting back to help Beth and Seb."

"Aye lass ,will ye save a dance for me after?"

"Yes of course."

"If there weren't sa many damned people around, I'd kiss ye. I love yer hair like that, it suits ye. Yer a very bonnie lass for all yer so modest about it."

She flushed with pleasure and squeezed his arm. "Thank you. If we're exchanging compliments, I must tell you that you look superb in a kilt, Doctor Thornton."

"I wore it for ye, lass. I'll wear it for our wedding too."

She closed her eyes and bit her lip. She must tell him the truth later, when they could find some time alone.

"Must ye look so pained lass? Yer doing my self-esteem no good at all!" His tone was gently teasing, but she wasn't fooled. Her continued prevarication was hurting him.

"Later," she murmured.

"I'll hold ye to that," he growled, kissing her hand and squeezing her fingers.

HE WATCHED her disappear into the throng and sighed. He had hoped after last night that he had at last broken through her defences, but he wasn't so sure.

While the supper was being served, he was cornered by Mrs Craig who reminded him of a rash promise he had made at one of the planning meetings for the fête.

"I think this will be the perfect time for your demonstration Doctor. What did you call it?"

He groaned inwardly and said in a hollow voice, "The Ghillie Callum. The Scottish sword dance. But I'll need two swords for it."

"No problem, I got them from Mitch earlier, before he got too drunk to stand."

"Where is he?" he asked quickly.

"Sleeping it off under a tree. Don't be concerned, I'm keeping an eye on him, and Mr Rooke will see him home later."

A few minutes later the swords were produced, and he placed them on the ground while the musicians assembled to play for him. It lacked bag pipes, but the fiddle and flute provided the right melody, and the supper chatter gradually quietened as he began the steps of the dance, he'd learned as a young lad. Being lighter on his feet than his brother, he'd taken to the dance and practised it. He was a bit rusty though and for a few moments he was afraid he wouldn't remember, but muscle memory kicked in and the rhythm took him back in time to his teen years when he'd been the champion Gillie Callum dancer in the village of Dysart. Another reason for his father's scorn.

"Dancing is for lassies, not men!" he berated. Merlow'd shrugged it off, more determined than ever to dance in the teeth of his father's opposition. Stubbornness ran in the family.

The music gradually sped up, as did his steps, until he was flying over the swords with kicks and flicks of his ankles and twists of his lower legs, his arms held high above his head. Fortunately, his daily practice of martial arts kept him both fit and flexible.

All the same, he was hot when he was done and panting for breath. Beth appeared with a welcome tankard, and he toasted the musicians and the company as they applauded and cheered. The band took their bows too, and he retired with his tankard to catch his breath and cool down.

HETTY FOUND him a little later with some supper to share, and he took heart from that.

"There is no end to your talents," she said taking a seat beside him on the trestle and offering the plate and fork. He took the fork and stuck it in a rissole.

"Thank yee lass, I was a bit rusty, but it all came back once I'd started. These are good," he said chewing.

"Beth made them," she said forking up some peas and mashed potato.

"Are ye happy with how it's gone?" he asked gesturing with his fork.

"I am. I don't know how much we have made yet, but I think it will be quite substantial. Certainly, enough to cover the repairs to the church we need to make, plus enough to keep in reserve in case of emergencies. It's definitely been our best year yet. The good weather has helped I think."

She signed leaning back, a hand to her stomach. "I'm full. Too much pecking at all the goodies on sale, people kept giving me tasters of their wares!"

He watched her with a softened heart. She was so unconsciously adorable he had to forcibly restrain himself from hugging her for sheer delight in her presence. *God, he loved her.*

"Yer the heart and soul of his village ye know. They all love ye." He spoke quietly, just for her ears. Wishing they were alone.

She opened her eyes and blinked, sitting up and blushing faintly. She was so modest and humble. "I'm just doing my job," she protested. "Helping Papa." She frowned a look of concern in her eyes. "I'm worried about him. He still hasn't fully recovered his strength. Do you think he ever will?"

"Hard to say lass," he said honestly. He wouldn't lie to her. "He seemed to be mending nicely the last time I gave him a check-up, what specifically concerns you?"

"He is still thin, and he tires more easily than he did before he got ill."

"It's only been a few weeks. He was very ill, likely it will take up to six months or more for him to get back to full strength. But yer right, he may never be as strong as he once was again. An illness like that can debilitate beyond the body's ability to full recover."

She blinked and wiped at her cheek. "He's not old!" she protested. "It's so unfair. He's such a good man, he doesn't deserve this!"

"I know, lass," he said taking her hand and

squeezing it for comfort. "Unfortunately, goodness doesn't appear t' be any protection against misfortune."

"I know!" she said sniffing. "I pray for him every night. I don't know how I'd cope if I lost him!"

"Aye love," he said his heart wrung for her and wishing he could put his arms round her and comfort her properly. "If it's any comfort, I do think he stands a good chance at a full recovery, provided he doesna contract anything else, while his body's still vulnerable."

She nodded and squeezed his hand back. "I will keep a better eye on him. Mrs Corcoran is feeding him well anyway. And I'll keep up my prayers."

The musicians started up again to herald the beginning of the dancing. The sun was now casting long shadows along the ground as the day began to close in. It being the height of summer it wouldn't be full dark for some hours yet.

"Care to dance, Hetty?" he asked.

"Yes, please Merlow," she said softly. The look she gave him sent his heart tripping. If he could just get her alone for a bit...

Rising, he led her onto the dance floor, a raised platform laid out in big squares on the grass for the occasion. The village carpenter had spent the last several months converting pallets into a suitable surface and using wooden pegs to slot them together. Many others joined them on the cramped surface.

Three dances later, he led her off the floor to make room for others waiting for a turn, and they wandered off to the field behind the Church which was now deserted. The sun was an orange ball of fire on the horizon, with the sky darkening above. The temperature was dropping, but it wasn't cold yet. The music and laughter of the revellers followed them, but finally they had a little privacy.

With his arm round her waist, he brought her to a stop and pulled her close.

"I've been dyin' to kiss ye all day," he said husky voiced, lowering his head to do so. She leaned into the kiss, to his delight, and several delicious moments later he broke the kiss reluctantly and squeezed her tight for sheer joy. "I love ye, Hetty!" he said unable to keep the words in. "And I'm sae proud of yer efforts, tis because of ye that today is such a success. Ye should be right proud of yerself."

"I had lots of help, including yours, when you have so little time-" she protested modestly.

"Ye canna take a compliment can ye lass?" He teased gently.

"Not when I don't deserve it!" she said somewhat more vehemently than the situation warranted.

"Now what maggots got into ye heid? Ye deserved to be buried in compliments."

She opened her mouth and closed it, as her eyes caught something. Turning, she pointed to the sky. "Oh look! It's a shooting star!"

He looked up and sure enough a bright streak of white light was arcing across the darkening sky above the blaze of colour nearer the horizon.

"Make a wish!" she said, closing her eyes.

"Aye lass!" he said clasping her hand in his. She squeezed his hand back, and he wished with all his might that she would trust him with her secret.

They stood silently a moment, watching the star as it faded from sight.

"Is it a good omen do you think?" she asked, finally breaking the silence.

"Aye lass, I hope so."

"Doctor Thornton!" a voice hailed him from the back of the church. It was Mrs Craig, hurrying towards them over the field. He stifled a sigh, so much for their privacy.

She reached them panting, her generous bosom heaving. "It's one of the O'Donnell boys, he's fallen out of tree and hurt himself."

"Where Mrs Craig?"

"Down by the river. You know what boys are, they slipped off when no one was looking!"

"I'll just get my bag it's at Mr Rookes stall. I was afraid we might get some injuries today. Coming Miss Rooke?"

"Of course," said Hetty.

"Sorry to interrupt your tryst Doctor," said Mrs Craig with a smirk. Hetty blushed. "But don't worry, I won't tattle!"

Oh, but she would! Not that it was news, everyone knew he was courting Hetty. Still to be found alone in a darkened field... Fortunately they weren't doing anything more compromising than holding hands. Good thing she hadn't caught them kissing!

CHAPTER 13

*D*urand entered the Bulls Head Tavern in Pinner and looked about. There were a few patrons having quiet ones at tables scattered about the room, but no sign of the publican.

"Yo! Tap!" he called, leaning on the bar and dropping his bag at his feet. He'd parted ways with General Ming on the outskirts of Pinner, the secretive Chinese unwilling to make his presence known to his quarry. Durand suspected the man was dangerous to the doctor and wondered if he should warn him? But all the evidence pointed to the fact that the doctor was perfectly capable of looking after himself.

"Coming!" said a deep voice from a room behind the bar and a huge, dark visaged man appeared in the doorway.

"Rooke!" Durand exclaimed, recognising his old school friend immediately. "What are you doing here?"

"I'm the Publican, what can I do for you?" the

man said, his eyes narrowing slightly in an effort of memory.

"You've forgotten my name, haven't you?" Durand accused him teasingly. He held out his hand "Durand Percival. I couldn't forget you, you great ox, you won every boxing bout and had the little fellows terrified."

"Percival!" Sebastian Rooke smiled in welcome. He indicated the bag at Percival's feet. "Are you staying?"

"Yes, if you have a room?"

"Aye we do," Seb pushed the register towards him and turned to fetch down a room key from the board behind the bar. "Are you staying long?"

"I might stay for a few days, maybe a week. Taking a break from London, on my way to a friend's place and thought I'd drop by and check out the old stomping ground. We used to go fishing in the river, remember?" Durand let the prattle roll off his tongue easily. He'd tagged along with Seb and his friends, because, despite appearances, at that age he hadn't been as confident or socially competent as he was now. The fact that he had outranked the other boys because his father was a viscount, had given him the edge, not that the others, including Seb, had seemed in the slightest bit impressed.

"I do," said Seb. "Would you care for luncheon?" he asked, checking the details in the register and handing Durand the key.

"I would, I'll just go freshen up and come back down."

"I'll let my wife know, she'll serve you when you're ready."

"You're married? I look forward to meeting your lady!" Percival said with a smile, masking a vague stab of jealousy. If that great ox could find a wife ,why couldn't he? He stifled the thought, he didn't need or want a wife, his life was quite enjoyable enough without the encumbrance of female company.

"We were married three months ago."

"Still in the honeymoon phase?" Percival cocked an eyebrow knowingly and picked up his bag. That would explain the besotted look that came over his face when he mentioned his wife. That would soon wear off. Durand experience of his parent's marriage did not fill him with romantic notions.

"You'll find your room on the left at the end of the passage," said Seb as he headed nonchalantly for the stairs.

"Thanks," Durand said, running lightly up the stairs, his bag over his shoulder.

SEB HEADED BACK to the kitchen and stuck his head through the door. Beth was cutting out rounds of pastry and lining little pie dishes with them.

"We have a guest who would like luncheon," he said with a smile as she blew a wisp of hair off her nose. "He's gone up to his room, but will be down shortly."

She wiped the back of her hand across her forehead. "I'll come out when I have these in the oven. Is there anyone else for luncheon?"

"O'Donnell and Beatson are having a quiet one in the corner, I'll ask them if they want to eat."

"Mr O'Donnell again?"

"Aye." Seb frowned. "He's not sodden yet."

"Have you thought of refusing to serve him?"

"Aye but he'll just go elsewhere if I refuse him. At least if he's here I can keep an eye on him."

She nodded and sighed.

He wandered back to the tap and strolled over to his two drinking customers. Just as he did so, the eldest O'Donnell child, Matthew, a young man of twenty came in, spotted his father and came over.

"Father, you have to come home!" Matt was a tall thin young fellow with a shock of untidy dark hair, that needed a cut. His clothes were ill-fitting and had patches on the elbows and knees. "Leave me be boy!" growled O'Donnell into his tankard.

Matt took a hold of his arm and tugged. "Mothers had a fall! She's bleeding! You need to come! Now!" Matt's normally pale face was red with frustration and anger.

His words seemed to penetrate O'Donnell's skull for he said, "Doctor been sent for?"

"Of course!" snapped Matt. "If you don't come now, I'll bar the house to you, and you can sleep in the bloody barn!"

This got O'Donnell on his feet, swaying slightly. "It's my house boy! I should clip you upside the head for your insolence!"

"You can try!" said Matt standing his ground.

O'Donnell blinked at him a moment and then his face crumpled. "I'm sorry lad, but you don't understand! It hurts mortal bad. Four! We lost four!"

Matt's face cracked. "Yes Papa, I know. But you'll lose a fifth if you don't come. Mama needs you!"

O'Donnell nodded. "You're right lad." He straightened and glanced sheepishly at Beatson and Seb. "I'll bid you good day." He turned to his son who took his arm.

Seb said quietly over his head to Matt, "you right with him?"

"Yes, thank you sir. Come on Papa." he wrapped an arm round his father and the two walked a little unsteadily out the door.

Seb turned back to Beatson, "Mr Beatson, would you care for luncheon?"

"Some of your lovely wife's cooking? Don't mind if I do, lad."

Seb suppressed a smile at being referred to as a lad. Came of being back in the town he was raised in. More than half the residents could remember him as a boy, and thus, despite his size, he would remain in their eyes.

"Beth will be out in a bit to take your order," he said, picking up O'Donnell's half empty glass and wiping down the table. "Found Fred a girlfriend yet?"

Beatson chuckled. "He has a whole paddock of girlfriends, lad. It's keeping him *out* of the cow's paddock that's the problem!"

DURAND, having unpacked his belongings and washed his face and hands, came back downstairs to the tap room, conscious of a growling stomach.

Rooke was headed back to the bar with an empty glass just as Percival appeared. Seb got him settled at a table, took his order for a drink and waved at the menu board on the wall.

"Beth will take your order shortly," he said. "Everything all right with the room?"

"Perfectly satisfactory thank you," Percival smiled determined to be a pleasant guest. His conscience was pricking him about Henrietta. Obviously, Seb didn't know what went on between them or he'd have planted Durand a facer on sight. *He couldn't help wondering how she was. Could he ask without raising any suspicions?* Two more customers wandered in just then, presumably signalling the start of the afternoon rush.

Mrs Rooke emerged shortly after that, drying her hands on her apron. She was a pretty little thing with blonde hair waving round her face and winsome smile. With stylus and wax tablet in hand, she began to circulate, taking food orders. She reached Durand's table and said, "and what can I get you to eat sir?"

Durand was conscious of Seb's eyes on them as he said with a smile of appreciation, "The tongue pie and cheese please. Do you make it yourself?"

"I do all the baking, sir, yes."

"Well, if the food is as delectable as you, I will be a happy man," he said outrageously. She was very young, as her blush and confusion at his compliment showed. *Really, how did Rooke get so lucky?*

Durand finished his ale, discovering that he was thirsty, and Seb appeared at his side.

"Another one?" he said picking up the empty.

"Yes, thank you, you lucky devil." He indicated with a nod to the kitchen what he was referring to. "Congratulations."

Seb grinned with obvious possessive pride.

"Where did you meet her?"

"In London. What do you plan to do while you're here?"

"Bit of fishing, maybe. I'm assuming there isn't a lot of night life here?" *Not unless things had changed dramatically in twelve years.*

"No, we hold a card night on Fridays for shilling points, but you'll have to go to Harrow for anything more exciting. There's a monthly assembly held in the hall at Harrow school. You might remember that from our own days? Most of the young ladies frequent that. I sometimes take Beth, it's on Wednesday night."

"Sounds like fun," quipped Percival, his fingers tapping on the table. "Speaking of young ladies, does your sister still live here?"

"Hetty still resides with our father at the Vicarage." Seb raised an eyebrow.

Durand's smile widened, hoping to deflect suspicion. "I must pop in and say hello, see if she remembers me."

"She's walking out with the doctor, expecting an announcement any day now," growled Seb, suddenly resembling a bulldog with a bone.

Percival nodded; his smile fixed to his lip and ignoring the don't touch her signals coming off the other man. "Good to know." *My God, Henrietta was being courted by the doctor? Was she in any danger? What a coil! Things just went from bad to worse!*

Mrs Rooke appeared then with a large slice of tongue pie with fresh crusty bread and butter a generous wodge of cheese.

Durand thanked her and cut into the pie; the first mouthful was indeed as delicious as it looked. *Seb was a very lucky sod.*

CHAPTER 14

*H*etty left the church hall and crossed the garden in front of the church towards the vicarage, her mind on her remaining tasks for the day.

"Good day Miss Rooke."

The voice behind her, sent a cold sluice down her back and arrested her steps. For a moment she forgot how to breathe. Then her heart kicked in, racing, and she turned slowly to confront the man she honestly thought she would never see again.

He smiled and stepped out of the lee of the Church porch and bowed politely.

"You're even prettier than I remembered."

Part of her was screaming to run, but she couldn't seem to move.

He stepped closer and took her hand, slipping it into his arm he tugged her to walk with him round the side of the hall, away from the street.

Her legs were trembling and felt numb.

He said conversationally, "I wanted to renew

our acquaintance, I'm glad to see you looking well my dear."

He came to a stop behind the hall and let her go. She stepped back and he stepped forward.

"You do remember me, don't you?" he said with a smile that made her stomach turn over.

She swallowed and found her tongue at last. "Of course I do. How do you do Mr Percival? What brings you to Pinner?"

"Why you do of course. I am on my way to visit friends and I couldn't resist the opportunity to come and check on your welfare."

"Why now, after all this time?"

"I confess I am embarrassed by my lack of finesse back then; my ignorance was appalling. If I recall you were somewhat upset, I must tender my apologies, I didn't mean to hurt you."

She gaped at him, so shocked by his view of what she recalled as her shame and horror. She had felt used and abused by him, but blamed herself for it. Knowing now, after Merlow's gentle handling, that things could be so much better between a man and a woman, somehow made it worse. *Didn't he understand he had ruined her? Wrecked her life? With his casual taking?*

"I was a feckless young sprig back then. It didn't occur to me at the time to be concerned for consequences. I gather there were none?"

"None visible to others, no," she said swallowing bile.

"You relieve my mind. I understand you are on the brink of receiving a marriage proposal."

"Who told you that?"

"Your brother of course. I asked after you and I

think he was warning me off. Not that he knows about our former - ah–friendship, does he?"

"No one knows," she said hoarsely. This was a nightmare, and she would wake up at any moment and find that she had fallen asleep in the hall over the church accounts.

"Certainly not your prospective bridegroom I gather. Doctor Thornton, is it?"

She shuddered. Her muscles were locked so tight she didn't think she could move, her tongue cleaved to the roof of her mouth. Her nightmare was coming home to roost. He would tell Merlow of her shame and her happiness would evaporate on the wind. Her heart felt as if it was breaking up inside her chest. It hurt so much she couldn't breathe.

When she didn't answer he went on with a little smile, "never mind I shan't tell him. No doubt he has secrets too, ones he wouldn't want you to know."

"W-what do you mean?" tentative relief that he didn't mean to destroy her happiness, tempered by his other words.

"Oh, nothing untoward, I'm sure." He smiled again, but she shuddered, she couldn't shake off the feeling that his smile was forced, not sincere. "Has he told you about his dealings with the Chinese?"

"He has told me about his travels, yes. To India and the West Indies as well as China." *What could he know of Merlow's past?*

He nodded thoughtfully. "Well, it has been a pleasure to see you again my dear," he took her hand and kissed it. "I wish you all the best with your doctor. But do get him to tell you about his dealings with the Chinese, a man capable of taking on three men at once and leaving two of them dead in a ditch is one with secrets to tell, I'm sure."

"What are you talking about?" Her heart sped up so fast it was like to leap from her chest, as a wash of cold horror cascaded over her skin. Merlow was a healer not a killer. She snatched her hand from his grip and took a step back. Her knees trembling, her breath coming in pants.

"It's not my secret to reveal my dear, but you might warn him he is in danger. If he doesn't surrender what he stole."

"You speak in riddles!" She said bewildered.

He bowed to her and walked away, leaving her stunned and shaking, her mind splintered, her heart aching.

DURAND WALKED AWAY from Henrietta Rooke more shaken than he wanted to admit. His memories of her had become fuzzy with time and she had been so much younger then. They both were. Seeing her again had brought back a flood of feelings he had thought long dead and buried. He had fancied himself passionately in love with her at the time, he'd learned after their disastrous coupling that his infatuation was driven in large part by youthful lust. Brought to his senses and thoroughly ashamed of himself, he'd fled and tried not to think about her ever since. Her pallor and shocked expression, the dark, wounded look in her eyes, told him he done more damage than he'd realised.

And she was walking out with Doctor Thornton. *What manner of man was he? He'd no way of telling. But anyone capable of leaving two men dead in ditch was surely dangerous and not someone a sweet woman like Henrietta should be involved with.* Yet how to protect her from him? He needed to meet this damned doctor and judge for himself if he was the right man for her. If not, he would have to intervene. He owed her that at the very least.

RELIEVED TO BE RID of the Englishman, Ming spent the day circling the small village of Pinner and locating the doctor's residence. He would strike when the sun went down.

CHAPTER 15

*M*erlow stepped into the tap room of the Bull's Head Tavern, and spotting Sebastian Rooke wiping down tables, crossed the room to his side. There were a few patrons partaking of porter or ale, talking quietly at their tables.

Sebastian took one look at his face and rumbled, "you need a drink."

Merlow scrubbed a hand through his hair. "Probably. I've just come from the O'Donnell's." He followed Sebastian to the bar where the big man poured him a tankard of dark porter.

"How is Mrs O'Donnell?" Sebastian put the tankard on the bar as Merlow sat down on a stool.

"Resting, I've got her eldest daughter watching her and she's to send for me if anything changes."

"The baby?"

"All right for the moment. I gather young Matt fetched his father from here?"

"Aye." Sebastian rubbed down the bar with a cloth. "Do you want me to refuse to serve him?"

"Ye may not have to. He's pretty shaken up about this morning. I think the message might have got through. Matt was quite blunt with him."

Sebastian nodded. "Aye he was when he was here. What actually happened?"

"Mrs O'Donnell tripped over something doing the laundry and fell. She started bleeding. Fortunately, not a lot and it seems to have stopped. She's confined to bed for a wee while, and I've given strict orders she's to be on light duties for the remainder of the pregnancy. O'Donnell was pretty remorseful when I left. Seems like this was the wake up call he needed." He took a long draft of the porter and wiped his moustache. "Wish he'd use the bluidy neem oil. It's a miracle the woman has survived this many pregnancies."

He sighed and rubbed his eyes; they were gritty from lack of sleep. Between worrying over Hetty and his patients and concern for whether he'd truly shaken off the Qing Agents on his tail, he was having restless nights.

"The other one I'm worried about is Stewart. Has he been in much?"

"Aye but only to buy liquor to take home."

"What's he drinking?"

"Whisky."

Sebastian nodded to someone over Merlow's shoulder, and he swivelled on the stool to see who. A man he didn't recognise sauntered across the floor heading for the stairs. He was tall, blonde and well-dressed. He glanced in Merlow's direction and looked away quickly as he placed a foot on the steps and ran up them lightly.

"A guest?" queried Merlow.

"Aye. School friend of mine, well acquaintance more than friend. Odd start of his to visit again after so many years. We were at Harrow together."

"How long since he was here?"

"Must be a dozen years or so." Sebastian frowned. "He asked after Hetty. I warned him she was spoken for."

Merlow set the tankard down slowly, his heart taking a tumble and beating hard with a sudden premonition. "Twelve years ago? Hetty would have been, what sixteen?"

Sebastian raised an eyebrow. "Aye. Why?"

"What's the fellows name?"

"Durand Percival. His father's a Viscount."

Merlow resisted asking for the man's room number, for one thing he had no proof of the suspicion forming in his mind and for another, Hetty wouldn't appreciate her brother being apprised of her secret. She had kept it to herself for a long time. If she had wanted her father or her brother to know, she would have told them.

He finished the tankard, contemplating how he might contrive to have a word with Mr Percival in private, and was about to pay for his drink and leave, when young Ben Nieves pelted through the door panting, "somebody help!"

Rising from his stool he said, "what is it boy?"

"Mr Stewart's trying to kill his self!"

"Where?"

"On the bridge."

Merlow ran with young Ben out of the tavern into the street, heading for the stone bridge over the river Pin, a hundred yards down the street. A moment later they were joined by Sebastian who had stayed momentarily to call his wife from the kitchen to mind the tap. Ben panted beside Merlow, "My da came across him with a lump of rock tied round him standin' on the bridge, he sent me to find someone to help, he was tryin' to restrain him when I left."

Merlow pelted down the road to the bridge. As the bend in the road revealed the road ahead, he could see a body lying in the middle of the bridge and another sitting on the rail nursing something in his lap. Mitch was a big man, like Seb, clearly Nieves was no match for him. Reaching the bridge he called out,

"Mitch! Dinnae do it man, Maggie wouldna want that!"

Mitch shook his shaggy, bearded head, and tipped forward into the water, letting the rock go as he did it. The rock dropped, jerking him downwards towards the water.

"Fook!" swore Merlow and climbing over the rail went in after him. The river wasn't all that deep, but it was deep enough to drown a man with a rock attached to him, especially if he couldn't swim.

Fortunately, Merlow *could* swim, being raised on the coast and spending many summers of his childhood playing in the water, paid off. He dived into the water from the bridge, just as Mitch Stewart's body hit the water with a splash and disappeared from view, dragged down by the rock attached to his waist.

The river water was cold and murky as Merlow entered it in a clean dive, and he turned, trying to find Mitch's body. The man was thrashing about, seeming the instinct for survival had kicked in, and Merlow caught his arm and tried to drag him towards the surface.

Mitch, in his panic, kept thrashing and kicked Merlow in the groin. Pain lanced through him, forcing him to the surface to gasp for air. Diving back down and ignoring the waves of pain arcing through his body, he grabbed Mitch again, his thrashing slowing, and fumbled for the knot tying the rope around his waist.

Reaching into his pocket he took out a knife and sawed through the rope. It took an agonisingly long time, as Mitch's body stilled and dragged, hanging heavy in his grip. The rope finally gave way, and he kicked hard for the surface. Getting Mitch's head above the water, he struck out for the bank where he found Sebastian waiting for him. Seb helped him pull Mitch's body onto the bank and Merlow checked his breathing.

He immediately began applying pressure to Mitch's chest and breathing into the other man's mouth. He kept this up for what seemed like an eternity, but in reality, could have only been a few minutes at most, until with a gasp and a choking cough, the other man began to breathe again. Rolling him onto his side as the drowned man coughed upriver water, he wiped water off his own face and rubbed the man's back as he heaved.

"That's it man! Get it all out."

Mitch, between heaving coughs, began to cry. Jumbled in the coughing and sobs Merlow made out the words, "Maggie! I'm sorry, Maggie!"

Merlow glanced up as he heard Hetty say, "Is he all right?"

"He will be," he said, wiping rivulets of water off his face from his hair. His clothing was soaked through, and a slight breeze made him shiver.

"Seb, is Nieves all right? I saw he was down but I dinnae have time to check on him."

"Aye," Sebastian nodded. Mrs Craig has his head in her lap. Merlow glanced around and realised that half the village was gathered on the bridge or on the riverbank. Hetty pushed her way through the crowd to his side and crouched down.

"Are you all right?" she asked quietly.

"Aye lass, just a wee bit wet," he said with a smile. The pain in his groin was subsiding. He bent over his patient. "Mitch? Can ye walk man, or do ye need Rooke to carry ye?"

Mitch gasped and said hoarse voiced, "Aye, I can walk."

Merlow helped him sit up and Mitch glanced round at the crowd and looked at him red eyed and sheepish. "Sorry doc."

"Aye well, we'll get ye home and dry." He nodded to Seb, who put his arms under the other man's pits and helped him rise. As they manoeuvred the man up the bank to the road, he noticed Percival hovering in the background. The man was staring at him rather hard and Merlow was conscious of his hackles rising. He glance about for Hetty, who was right beside him. She seemed unaware of Percival's scrutiny. He wanted to wrap his arms round her in a show of possessiveness, but the circumstances made that impossible. He gave her a smile instead and she smiled back. He glanced back at Percival, but the man had dropped out of sight.

Twenty minutes later, Mitch was tucked up in bed with the doctor sitting beside him. He'd sent Hetty to find someone to sit with him, he shouldn't be left alone; and Seb to fetch his doctor's bag, from which he'd produced a tincture of St John's Wort to add to the man's cup of tea.

"Yer to take this daily, ye understand?" he said waving the bottle.

Mitch nodded. "Sorry Doc," he said again.

Merlow shook his head. "Don't be sorry, just don't do it again. If it gets that bad come find someone to talk to. Maggie wouldna want ye te do that, ye know she wouldn't."

Mitch looked into his teacup and swallowed. "I just can't abide the pain Doc. I miss her so!" Tears welled and ran down his cheeks.

"I know man. Ye realise ye kicked me in ballocks while ye were thrashing aboot?"

"Nay!" The other man's mouth fell open in shock.

"Thought I was done for meself for a moment or two, hurt like the very devil!"

Mitch's lips twitched, which was the reaction Merlow was hoping for. He'd never met a man yet, that could remain straight-faced at the prospect of another man getting a wallop in the cods.

By the time Hetty reappeared with Mrs Craig, both men were in gusts of laughter, with tears streaming down their cheeks. The two women looked at each other as if they had run mad.

"Care to share the joke?" asked Hetty.

"Ye wouldna understand lass," he said wiping his eyes.

. . .

LEAVING Mrs Craig with instructions on how to care for her patient, Hetty allowed Merlow to escort her back to the Vicarage. Her interview with Mr Percival burning in her breast. *Should she say anything? And if so, what?* Cravenly she took refuge in the immediate instead.

"It was good to see Mr Stewart laughing, but what was so funny?"

"Ye really want to know?" He looked down at her, his grey eyes dancing with laughter.

"Yes, I do." She would get to the bottom of one secret at least.

He grinned. "When he was thrashing about in the water Mitch kicked me in the cods, it hurt like hell too."

She looked at him mystified. "And this is funny, how?" So much for unravelling secrets.

"I told ye, ye wouldna understand lass. It's a male thing, take my word for it."

She shook her head. Which made him laugh and slip his arm round her waist, pulling her off the side of the road into the lee of a tree.

"Kiss me Hetty, I need some comfort."

"You're still wet," she objected with a smile, letting him pull her close. Mr Percival's words faded as he bent his head and kissed her, the damp heat of his body soaking into her own clothes. She reached up behind his neck and surrendered to the bliss that was a kiss from Merlow. *Percival's words made no sense. Merlow was neither a murderer, nor a thief, she would swear to it. There must be some other explanation.*

A breeze stirred the leaves above their heads, and she felt a tremor pass through Merlow's body.

"You need to get out of those wet clothes before you catch a chill!" she scolded, pulling back.

He smiled ruefully, "while I'd like to say ye keep me warm, ye're right."

"I'll come with you," she said firmly. "There are some things I need to talk to you about."

His smiled widened and he pressed his lips to her forehead with a murmured, "I love ye Hetty."

CHAPTER 16

*H*etty *swallowed, would he still love her once she told him the truth?* She stiffened her backbone and stepped out beside him as they traversed the short distance back to the surgery. Unlocking the door, he let her in, locked the door behind them and setting his bag down on the side table, led her through to his private rooms behind the waiting room, consultation room, surgery and compounding room that took up most of the ground floor of the house.

"This is the sitting room," he said opening the door on the right. "And this is the kitchen," he said indicating the arch way that lead into the kitchen and pantry with a door leading out to the rear yard. "I'll just go up and change. If ye'd like to put the kettle on? I won't be long."

"Of course," she smiled and watched him ascend the small circular staircase tucked into the rear wall of the tiny vestibule she stood in. Going into the kitchen, she set about making tea and even found a tin with a few biscuits from the last batch she had given him. Loading all this onto a tray, she took it through to the sitting room and had it all set out and ready and a fire lit in the grate, when he reappeared, his hair tousled dry and dressed in clean, dry clothes.

He hadn't bothered with a neck cloth, or jacket, his shirt open at the neck. If she wasn't going to marry him, this would all be shocking, but she had made up her mind to confess everything and hope that he would still have her when she was done with her tale.

She pushed Mr Percival's strange words away. Time enough to address those when she had unburdened herself.

He took a cup of tea from her and sitting in the other armchair, he only had the two, he sighed. "This is so good, thankye."

She smiled and stirred sugar into her cup, wondering nervously where to begin. He reached for a biscuit. "You said you wanted to talk to me?" he prompted.

Taking a deep breath and clenching her hands tightly in her lap she nodded. "I do. You wanted me to tell you why I-" she swallowed. "Why I refused to marry." Her cheeks flooded, and she dropped her eyes, unable to look at him as shame engulfed her. With her heart thudding hard in her breast, she went on doggedly. "I must tell you that I am not–pure." She licked her lips. "I'm not the saintly vicar's daughter everyone thinks I am. I am a fallen woman. So, you see-" She stopped because he had put down his cup, got up and knelt at her feet.

"Look at me Hetty," he said gently.

She swallowed and raised her head so that she

was looking directly into his eyes. He placed his hands over hers. "Tell me the rest," he said with an encouraging look. There was no condemnation in his eyes, only a tender glow that made her heart swell and gave her courage.

"I-" she blinked and wiped away a tear. "It was a few days before my sixteenth birthday. I- it's no excuse, but I thought I was in love!" She swallowed again, wiping another tear away for her foolish sixteen-year-old self.

"How old was he?" Merlow's voice lowered, and her heart skipped, but she had begun now and couldn't stop until the tale was told.

"Nineteen, twenty, I'm not sure."

He nodded.

"I thought he loved me too, but-" she took a breath and let it out. "I was young and foolish."

"Did he force you Hetty?"

"N-no." She dropped her eyes, her cheeks flooding, for this was the heart of her shame. "I was willing. It was my fault!" She said in a heated rush. Her stomach muscles pulled tight, condemning herself for her idiocy.

"Did he hurt you?"

Tears gathered and spilled down her cheeks, recalling the pain, but more the stinging shame of it afterwards. "Yes. It hurt. It wasn't romantic or sweet or any of the things I thought it would be." She summoned a watery smile, a flood of warmth in her heart as she looked into his eyes. "It wasn't like it is with us."

He squeezed her hand and kissed it. She noticed his eyes glistening and his smile was wobbly. "Were there any consequences?"

"No. I was lucky. I–I thanked God for that and prayed for forgiveness. I tried so hard to atone for my wickedness." She shook her head. The shame of it overwhelming her again. "I don't deserve you!" She admitted the hot truth, her tears spilling over in a gushing rush and sobs clogging her throat as her heart twisted with pain.

He engulfed her in a hug, pulling her close. "Yes, you do my brave girl! Yes, you do!" He showered kisses on her hair, and she clung to him and cried until the sobs ran out, and then she just hung limp in his arms sniffing damply against his shirt.

The relief to have shared her burden, and not to be rejected for it, almost made her dizzy. She should tell him how she felt too, he deserved that. Yet Mr Percival's words echoed in her head, *was he lying? Making up stories to frighten her? By why would he do that? And what did his sinister warnings really mean?* She couldn't believe such tales of Merlow... yet he had admitted himself he would kill the man who hurt her. *Was he capable of such violence?*

ABOVE HER HEAD, Merlow sniffed and swallowed, relief, joy and pain warring for the upper hand. Pain at what she had been subjected to, relief that it had not been as bad as he had feared, and joy that she had finally trusted him enough to tell him the truth.

Was it a coincidence that she had chosen to tell him now, when Seb's school friend had suddenly appeared? *What was his name? Percival...* A man who was here twelve years ago, who would have been around twenty himself...

Merlow's stomach muscles tightened. She hadn't told him the man's name, and he was strangely reluctant to ask her. By her version of events there was no rape, just ineptitude and the sort of thoughtless selfishness young men were capable of. But the damage he'd wrought on Hetty was hard to forgive and Merlow itched to hurt him for it.

She had been brave enough to confess her secret; was he brave enough to confess his? She deserved the truth, but he flinched from the notion that she might be repelled by what he had to say, be horrified, as any gently reared woman would be, by the brutal reality of what he was capable of.

He recalled her recoil when he had indicated he would murder the man who hurt her, if he could.

Rising he pulled her up with him and took her place on the chair tugging her down onto his lap. She nestled in happily enough, resting her head on his shoulder and that encouraged him.

"Hetty I've a mite of confessing to do myself, will you hear me out lass?"

"Of course, but-" she hesitated.

"What is it love?"

She shook her head. "Nothing. Go on."

He snugged her closer against him and began. "You recall I've mentioned my Master Zhanghu-Zi a few times?"

She nodded. "He taught you Chinese medicine?"

"Yes, and also a style of fighting and moving meditation called Tai Chi. Do you understand what I mean by meditation?"

"Not really."

"It is a kind of restful contemplation."

"Like prayer?"

"That is probably the closest equivalent. But in the higher forms of meditation the objective is to clear and still the mind. To banish thoughts and remain in a state of stillness of the spirit. It is extremely difficult to do. I confess, even after years of practice I am still not very good at it. Zhanghu-Zi was very advanced.

"I think I told ye that he saved my life when I fell ill of a fever. When I recovered, I decided to stay and study with him. I became his apprentice if ye will. He inculcated me into not only medicine and Tai Chi but also the Dao. It means 'The Way', it is a form of religious philosophy. A guide to one's way of life, forms of thinking, daily practice. There are many flavours of it taught in China and Zhanghu-Zi was a proponent of the Baguadao, the Eight Trigrams Sect, a network of practitioners of the Dao that adhered to the tenets of the White Lotus."

She blinked up at him, bewildered by so many foreign terms.

"Never mind the details love, the point is Zhanghu-Zi was a leader of his branch of the Eight Trigrams and when the Sect decided to lead a rebellion against the Qing Government he joined the fray. Their forces attacked the Forbidden City. It was a mad undertaking, but he wouldna be persuaded not to do it. I learned that he was killed in the attack, some weeks later. It was a senseless waste in my view, and I was angry, and grief stricken by his loss. He had been the father of my spirit, and I was a better man for knowing him."

He stopped a moment, his throat tight and wiped his eyes, sniffing. Truthfully, he had cried more for Zhanghu-Zi's death than his own father's.

Hetty gripped his hand tightly in silent understanding, and he kissed her hair.

"I'm sorry for your loss," she whispered.

"Thankye, love." He held her close a moment and contemplated Zhanghu-Zi as he remembered him. The man was not large in stature, yet his spirit occupied a whole room, even though he barely said a word. His eyes were full of deep wisdom and his body was as strong as steel and supple as bamboo. His manner was gentle and yet fierce, his fighting techniques lethal. Yet he taught gentleness, forgiveness and a deep and abiding love for nature and humanity.

Just then she looked up at him and the temptation to kiss her overcame him. Cupping her face with his hand, he bent his head and kissed her soft lips. She shifted in his lap to angle her head for better contact, and he lost himself in the heat and comfort of her mouth.

She still hadn't said she loved him yet. He needed to hear the words from her. *How could he coax them out of her, and what was holding her back from uttering them?*

He broke the kiss, stroking a hand down her back, looking for the right words–when a thunderous knock on the front door made them both startle.

"What now?" he muttered as Hetty rose hastily off his lap and followed him as he headed to the front door.

He wrenched the door open and was startled to

see Percival standing on the doorstep. Hetty's gasp behind his left shoulder wasn't lost on him, and he stiffened protectively.

"Yes?" he said with a kind of growl.

Percival smiled as if he hadn't heard the growl and held out a hand. "Pardon the intrusion old chap I know we haven't been formally introduced. Percival is the name."

Ignoring the hand, Merlow said, "what do you want?"

"Wondered if I could have a word? In private?"

Reluctantly Merlow held the door open and shut it behind Percival after he stepped over the threshold.

Percival bowed to Hetty who flushed. "Miss Rooke."

She bobbed a curtsy but ignored Percival's hand.

"Well?" prompted Merlow.

"In private old chap?" suggested Percival with a faint flush.

"Whatever you have to say can be said in front of Miss Rooke."

Percival shrugged. "Very well. Just came to warn you, fellow by the name of Ming on your tail, pretty keen to ah obtain something in your possession," he said with a meaningful look.

Merlow frowned, his heart rate going up. *Another Qing agent?* "How do ye come to know of this?"

"Private word?" Percival tried for the third time.

With a growl, Merlow opened the door to his consulting room and waved the man in, he pushed the door to, but not shut. "What the bluidy hell are ye on about man? Out with it, before my patience runs oot!" His accent thickening with his annoyance.

Durand raised his hands placatingly. "I've been chasing you all the way from Dysart," he said. "I can see ill temper runs in the family." *Was he wrong? Was this man a danger to Hetty? But he'd seen him save that man's life, and he was a doctor.*

Merlow raised his eyebrows. "Ye met my brother?"

"I did." *And a surly SOB he was too!*

"Why?"

"Looking for you." *I said that didn't I?*

"I repeat, why?" *Time to execute his errand and get out of here.*

Durand reached into his pocket and drew out an envelope, which he passed over to Merlow. "To give you this."

Merlow turned it over and read the seal on the back. *His Majesties Government.* Frowning at Percival, he broke the seal and read the letter from the Prime Minister. Looking up, he folded the letter up. "I'm sorry to say ye have wasted yer time. I'm in expectation of getting married shortly, accompanying the Embassy to China is out of the question."

Before Durand could answer, Hetty pushed the door open and said, "Why?"

Merlow looked at her flummoxed. "I can't drag ye all the way to China, it's far too dangerous and I'm not leaving ye behind!"

Hetty flushed and moved to his side, placing a

hand on his arm. "But I would love to come. Why could we not go?"

Embarrassed Durand looked away during this passage, feeling decidedly *de trop. The sooner he left the better. Hetty was in good hands with this man. Despite his violent tendencies.*

MERLOW LOOKED DOWN into her face raised to his, her eyes sparkling. "Please Merlow?"

He wasn't proof against that. "I'll consider it," he said roughly.

Percival coughed. "I'll let you discuss it, shall I?"

"Before you go, I want to know more about this Ming."

"I ran into him in Dysart, he was looking for you. Seems you - ah - bested his men?" Percival said with a delicate raise of his eyebrows. "He is anxious to speak with you. We found his men where you left them."

Merlow's heart sank. At least Percival had some tact about him. "Hetty love would ye make us a cup of tea?" he asked with a smile.

She looked at him and at Percival and for a moment he thought she might refuse. His ruse to get her out of the room was transparent at best. She smiled, raised up on tip toe to kiss his cheek, "of course." Then she murmured, "don't hurt him," and left the room.

Which was a clear admission that Percival was the man who hurt her all those years ago. He clenched his fists and glowered at the Englishman. He must have looked fierce because Percival recoiled and moved strategically behind a chair.

"Tell me about yer association with Ming," growled Merlow, battling the urge to reach out and strangle the man. If Hetty weren't in the house, he probably would.

"He forced me to travel with him to find you. One of his men escaped your attack and found him in Dysart."

Merlow's heart sped up, *then the other man survived.*

"He died in the street in Ming's arms from his wounds."

Percival's words cut like a knife, dealing a blow to Merlow's solar plexus, more powerful than a slam to the chest. He actually staggered slightly and caught hold of the door to keep himself upright.

"Are you all right man?" asked Percival clearly alarmed.

Merlow closed his eyes and breathed. "I will be in a moment. Go on with your story." He swallowed. *He would deal with this later. It was important to listen to Percival's words and get him out of the house, preferably before Hetty came back.*

"We followed his men who were tailing you until just outside of Oxford when the trail went cold. Ming found his men in the ditch. He cremated them, said it would free their spirits or something. He surmised they had failed in their mission and took their own lives."

Merlow nodded. "Ming is a Qing agent?"

"He is a former General in the Qing military, that is all I know, he doesn't talk much."

"Why did you want to warn me about him?"

"Because I had a mission to perform, which I

167

have now discharged," he nodded to the envelope. "Ming's business with you is no concern of mine."

Merlow nodded thoughtfully. "Do you know where he is?"

"Somewhere nearby, we parted ways just outside of Pinner. I imagine he will visit you soon."

Merlow frowned. He didn't want Ming anywhere near Hetty, he had no way of knowing what the Chinese man might do, he must be desperate indeed to follow him all this way. And if he knew he was responsible for his men's death... He swallowed again the pain in his chest made it hard to breathe. He shook his head trying to clear it to think.

That the Qing Government were *this* determined to recover and destroy the sacred text made him all the more determined to preserve it in honour of his master's memory. It also made it impossible for him to contemplate returning to China if the Qing were so bent on its destruction.

"Thankye for the information," Merlow said grudgingly. "I hope ye mean to leave Pinner soon?"

"I do."

"Good. Ye know I that I know ye hurt Hetty, don't ye?"

Percival changed colour, losing his air of savoir faire. "I was young and ignorant. Believe me I regret it. I'm ashamed of myself. I tried to apologise to her."

Merlow nodded. "I'd like to darken yer daylights for ye, but Hetty wouldna like it. Best if you leave now."

Percival nodded and turned aside. "You'll consider the Embassy role?"

"Aye." *No need to inform Percival he couldn't take it. The man was obviously unaware of what Ming's actual object was. Better that he stay ignorant.*

He shut the front door on Percival just as Hetty reappeared with the tea tray.

"Oh, he's gone?"

"Aye lass, we'll have to drink the tea ourselves."

She looked at him knowingly over the tray. "You didn't hurt him I hope?"

"I was sorely tempted, but nay I did not."

CHAPTER 17

*H*etty carried the tea tray back to the sitting room and set it on the table. Straightening, she felt Merlow's arms come round her from behind, and pull her back against him.

"I confess, love," he said nuzzling her neck, "I'd rather have ye, than tea, right now."

"Oh Merlow," she sighed, leaning back against him. She let him kiss her neck and her ear and shivered with delight as heat flared along her nerve endings at his touch. Turning within his arms she wrapped hers round his neck and holding his eyes she said steadily, "you do know I love you, don't you?"

"Well, I was hoping ye did, but ye haven't ever actually said..."

"I adore you Merlow Thornton, and I would be over the moon with happiness to be your wife, if you'll have me?"

"Have ye? God in heaven Hetty, I've been wanting ye since I first laid eyes on ye. I'd be honoured beyond measure to call ye my wife. I've only asked ye a dozen times, ye stubborn wench!" He pulled her close and kissed her with a thoroughness that left her breathless and weak-kneed.

"Will ye come upstairs with me Hetty?" he said softly against her ear. "I'll not do anything ye don't want, I promise. I just want to hold ye, my precious darling."

She stared up at him, taking in the warm glow in his dear grey eyes, and her heart spilled over with love. "Yes," she whispered. "Oh, yes please, Merlow."

He led her up the narrow circular stair, where he unlocked the door of his bedchamber and held it open for her. The room had plain solid furniture, a large bed, dresser, robe, bedside table and a single chair before the fireplace. A window in the far wall showed the late summer sun as it headed for the horizon, casting a long orange glow across the floor and the bed. He sat down on the bed to remove his shoes and patted the space beside him.

With fast beating heart she sat gingerly beside him and let him put an arm round her waist. He cupped her face and kissed her, as she let herself get lost in his kisses. Gradually he eased her down onto the coverlet, and they lay face to face, kissing, hands moving lightly over each other. Tingling heat between her legs made her eager for more.

He must have sensed this, because shifting his weight, he pressed her back into the pillows, deepening his kisses, his lips running down her neck and across her collarbone, his hand cupping and squeezing one breast, making her whimper and arch her back. Heat and throbbing need made her run her hands over his back, pulling him closer.

"Merlow," she said breathlessly.

"Yes love?" he raised his head to gaze down at her, his weight on one arm.

"Will you take your shirt off?"

He grinned and reached behind his head to tug his shirt off. Pulling it clear he tossed it aside. "That what you want love?"

She nodded, taking in the glory of him, her hands going tentatively to touch the dark brown curls on his chest, the dying sunlight burnished them copper. Her fingers caught in the crinkly hairs covering the muscles on his chest like a pelt. She was seized with the absurd desire to rub her cheek over it like a cat. Flushing at her own thoughts she ran her hands over him his flesh, warm and resilient under her touch, the hairs course and soft at the same time. Leaning up she pressed a kiss to the base of his throat and then a series along his collarbone to the curve of his shoulder.

It was then she saw the tattoo on his upper arm. A strange abstract design in red, encased within a circle.

"What is this?" she asked tracing it with her fingertip.

"It's the symbol of the White Lotus. It indicates I am a student of the Baguadao."

"Oh, did it hurt?"

"Not a great deal."

She nodded and kissed it lightly, turning her attention back to his chest, which fascinated her. Resuming her kissing of his collarbone and throat, she worked her way from one shoulder to the other.

He made a muffled sound in his throat at this treatment, and she pushed him gently onto his back so that she could lean over him and run her face and her lips all over his chest in an orgy of delight.

"Hetty," his voice a soft growl. "That feel's wonderful love."

She raised her head a moment to smile and then leaned down to kiss him. His hands clamped onto her back pressing her close, as the kiss became deeper and more passionate. She broke it, to rub her face in his beard, and run her lips down his neck and to his chest again, his body hair an aphrodisiac she couldn't get enough of.

"May I loosen yer bodice Hetty?" he asked hoarse voiced.

"Yes," she said, breathless between kisses.

She felt his hands working at the laces on the back of her dress and the loosening of the neckline and bodice on the gown as he pulled the laces free. He pushed the shoulders of her gown down her arms as she sat up to help him, pulling the sleeves completely free and allowing her bodice to fall to her waist, revealing her corset and chemise. The corset sat below her breasts, half cups supporting them and leaving the nipples revealed through the semitransparent fabric of her fine cotton chemise.

His hands cupped them and squeezed, his fingers teasing her nipples and that rush of tingling heat between her legs intensified. "Ye're beautiful Hetty," he whispered. His hands reached up to pull the remaining pins from her half-undone bun, causing her hair to cascade heavily round her shoulders. Then he reached behind, to unlace her corset and pull it free. The removal caused a rush of cool air against her heated skin through the damp chemise. She sighed with the freedom to breathe easily and leaned closer as his hands returned to cupping and squeezing her nipples.

He pushed her chemise down, and she let it drop free of her arms leaving her breasts finally revealed fully to his gaze.

He groaned softly and leaned forward to suckle one pink tipped breast. A sharp bolt of heat arrowed from the touch of his tongue running over her nipple to the place between her legs. His hand pressed between her shoulder blades as she arched her back with a low moan.

Rising up, he pushed her gently down into the pillows and traced his lips across the tops of her breasts into her cleavage and then to the other nipple he hadn't tasted yet. The pull of his mouth on it was echoed between her legs again, and she whimpered with the sheer delight of it.

He pulled her skirts up, running a hand up her inner thighs, and she let her legs fall open for him, eager for the magic of his touch. His fingers caressed her gently and the sharp tingle made her breath catch.

He raised his head to watch her expression as his finger speared her lips and rubbed gently up and down the slippery channel between them.

She arched her back with a shameless moan. It felt so good and the freedom from guilt and shame made it even better.

"That's it love. Take yer pleasure!" he urged her roughly. His touch still delicate and light, gentle and persuasive, as he circled the entrance to her body with his finger, his thumb pressing gently and obliquely on that place of ultimate sensitivity as he slid his finger inside her.

She gasped with the shock of it, his thumb a teasing pleasure for her body, as his finger moved in and out, making her moan and thrash restlessly, her hips jerking.

"Merlow!" she whimpered.

"I know love!" he said softly. "Take yer pleasure ,sweetheart."

He pushed a second finger inside her and hooked them rubbing a spot inside her that sent a jolt of intense pleasure through her that made her cry out. He sped up the rotation of his thumb and the coiled heat inside her rose and rose, winding tighter and tighter until it suddenly burst with waves of exquisite delight. She gasped and moaned, her whole body going taught with it a moment as she trembled with the intensity of her release. Then melting into the bed as the waves washed through her, pulsing beats of intense bliss, breaking and ebbing slowly, winding down with her heart rate to a slow, heavy beat.

He pulled his fingers out gently and held her close as she came back to herself gradually. Stroking her back, he cradled her against him, her cheek resting on his chest.

"Merlow, you spoil me," she murmured, rubbing her cheek into his fur.

"You deserve to be spoilt love," he whispered, kissing her hair.

"So do you," she said, stroking his cheek. "Let me...?" She realised her ignorance was so vast she didn't even really know what she was offering.

.   .   .

MERLOW SMILED at her blush and a euphoric rush of love and relief coursed through him. It seemed he had slayed the beast of her past shame. She trusted him truly now. She was embracing pleasure as she should and in her usual selfless fashion, she was eager to return the gift of pleasure he had given her.

"Aye if ye like love," he said, reaching for the buttons on his breeches.

"I don't quite know what to do," she confessed with a rueful scrunch of her mouth. "You'll have to show me."

"I'll be glad to lass, to be honest me balls are blue!" he said with a slight grimace, as he freed his stiff cock from his breeches.

"Oh!" she said staring at it. "It's quite large isn't it."

His lips twitched, and he tried not to laugh at her awestruck expression. At least she didn't appear to be afraid. "No more than average lass," he said modestly.

"I supposed that is why it hurt so much," she said thoughtfully.

"It hurt because he was an ignorant lout and didn't prepare ye properly." he said roughly. "The first time will generally be a mite uncomfortable for a woman but it shouldna hurt to the degree you were hurt love."

"Oh."

"It won't hurt when we're joined sweetheart. I'll see to that. Ye felt how slippery ye were when I put my fingers inside ye? That didn't hurt, did it?"

"No."

"That's the state ye need to be in to receive me comfortably. Ye ken?"

She nodded.

He reached over to the bedside table and fetch the little pot of unguent he kept there and presented it to her. "Ye need to put a bit of this on yer hand to ease the stroke, in place of yer natural fluids. Otherwise, my cocks like to get a wee bit chafed."

"I see," she said removing the lid and smearing some on her palm. "Like this?" she asked, taking his cock gingerly in her hand and rubbing the ointment around the shaft.

He groaned softly at the pleasure of her touch. "Aye, pull the foreskin down and apply it on the head in particular, that's the most sensitive part, ye ken."

She applied a bit more cupping the head in her palm and sliding it around in a motion that made his stomach muscles clench with a groan. "Yes love!" he said breathlessly. Closing his eyes he said, "Stroke up and down, yes like that, a tad firmer—that's—that's good Hetty -" he groaned again. "Very good," he panted, thrusting his hips up into her grip, the urgent heat too much to resist. "Faster love," he begged. "Not going to last..." He disintegrated into Gaelic as the heated rush engulfed him. His balls contracted and the seed erupted from his cock onto his belly in hot spurts of intense pleasure. His muscles clenched, forcing groans from his throat, as the tension of days was released with the speed of a contracting spring.

"Fook!" he muttered with his eyes closed, his

breathing and heart rate racing, and descending slowly.

"Did I do it right?" she asked anxiously, and he opened his eyes and smiled at her.

"Yes love, normally it takes longer than that, but I was a wee bit overwrought." He reached for a handkerchief and wiped his belly.

The sun had dropped, leaving them in the gloaming, the long twilight of late summer. He pulled her close, "I'd best take ye home before yer father sends out a search party for ye."

"Yes, I suppose so."

"I'll ask him to put up the bans, yes?"

She nodded and smiled, linking her hand with his.

He kissed her hand and squeezed it. "I cannae wait to be joined with ye Hetty."

She sat up, pulling up her chemise, and he helped her lace up her corset and gown. She got off the bed and shook out her gown as he reached for his shirt and pulled it over his head, tucking it into his breeches and rebuttoning them. They each found their shoes, and she tried to repin her hair. When she had a semi-respectable chignon, she turned back to him and wrapped her arms round his middle, resting her head against his shoulder.

"I'm so happy Merlow, but there is one more thing..."

"Aye, what is that, love?" he asked his heart jerking in surprise.

She raised her head and looked up at him a slight frown between her brows.

"Mr Percival warned me that you were in some

kind of danger. I didn't understand what he was talking about. He accused you of things that-"

"Ah! I wish he hadn't told ye."

"Told me..." she faltered. "It's not true...?"

"Depends on what he told ye love?"

"You're not a murderer or a thief!" she said hotly. "I'd stake my life on that!"

He squeezed her close. "God, I love you woman!" his voice thickened with emotion. "I'd never take a man's life intentionally lass, but I can understand that it must have looked that way to him."

His guilt over the deaths of the three Qing warriors chewed at him. But he was clear headed enough to realise that the three of them had died because of their own actions as much, if not more than anything he had done. If the other man had not run off but let him treat his wound, he wouldn't have died. If the other two had not taken those pills...

He drew her down onto the bed again and proceeded to tell her the whole truth about the Chinese men who had tailed him from Fife, and the fourth man, Ming, who was still looking for him.

"I'll admit I'm concerned for yer safety love; those men were trained fighters, and this Ming is, I assume, the same. I have something he wants. In the name of my master, it's not something I wish to surrender, but if comes to a choice between yer safety and it, I know what I will choose. Ye need to understand I'll do anything to keep ye safe. Yer the sun and the moon to me Hetty. Nothing means more to me that ye."

She stroked his cheek, "I feel the same way.

Please be careful, don't put yourself in danger, I've only just found you, I couldn't bear to lose you now!" Her eyes glinted with moisture in the fast-fading light.

"I can take care of myself Hetty, don't fret. I'll rid us of this problem as fast as I can, but ye see, if the Qing Government is after this text and me, I won't be able to accept the commission to join the Embassy."

"Yes, I understand. Oh well, it would have been exciting to go but I can see that it wouldn't be safe for you."

"It wouldn't be safe for either of us." He rose, "Come, I'll take ye home and speak to yer father."

He held the door for her, and she stepped out into the hallway heading for the stairs as he closed and locked the bedroom door behind him, for it was where the precious Neidan text and sword were stashed under the floorboards beneath the bed.

A muffled squeak from Hetty made him turn, and cold horror sluiced down his spine. A tall Chinese man in tunic, pants and a long leather coat, stood at the top of the stairs with Hetty held against his chest and knife at her throat.

CHAPTER 18

"Give me the text and the sword, or I will take her life in payment for the lives of my men you stole!" the Chinese said.

Hetty struggled at this and Merlow said sharply, "Hetty, stay still. He won't hurt you if I give him what he wants. Will you?" he addressed the man he assumed was Ming.

"Bring them," Ming said, edging backwards towards the top of the stairs.

"Where are ye taking her!" Alarm made Merlow's voice rise.

"Bring them to the stand of trees by the river." Ming addressed him in Chinese this time.

"Don't hurt her!" Merlow's response in English was to reassure Hetty, whose pallor and expression of terror were tearing him apart. "I will bring them. Don't hurt her!"

Ming's grunt was all the reassurance he got as the Chinese manoeuvred Hetty down the stairs and out the front door. Merlow had to physically stop himself chasing after them, which was his first instinct, and instead retrace his steps to the bedroom door.

Unlocking it took longer, because his hands were shaking so much. Never in his life had he felt so afraid. With the door open, he rushed to push the bed aside to get to the loose floorboards beneath and extract the text and the sword. Rushing downstairs, he grabbed a knife from the compounding room and slipped it into his boot. It was a long bladed and very sharp knife for cutting, better than no weapon at all. Not stopping to lock the house, he ran across the road and up to the common, towards the spinney. The sun had gone by now and it was full dark, the only light from a rising moon.

He headed for the spinney, entering the shadowed canopy of their branches, the leaf mulch soft under foot. He recalled with vivid detail the night he had brought Hetty here. It seemed ironic. He called out, "Ming, I have the things you want, let her go!"

"Merlow!"

Hetty's shriek, shaking with fear, tore a hole in his chest and told him which way to go. His heart thudding so hard it threatened to leap from his body, he plunged further into the stygian dark of the trees, only broken by patches of silvery moonlight when there was a gap in the canopy.

"If ye hurt her Ming, I'll kill you!" he shouted, his control snapping.

His senses on high alert, he caught the rustle of footsteps on the mulch to his right and stopped to pinpoint their direction. He caught a glimpse of movement and ran towards it. The trees opened out into a clearing in the middle of which stood Ming, still holding Hetty, that deadly knife to her throat. She appeared unhurt, but her face was pale, and her eyes shadowed.

Merlow came to a stop and held out the text and the sword. "I have what you want, let her go!"

"Put them over there," Ming nodded with his head to a raised stone with a flat top, to the right and about halfway between himself and Merlow.

Merlow nodded. "All right." He stepped towards the rock, keeping his eyes firmly fixed on Ming. He set down the sword and the text slowly and backed away.

Ming jerked his head. "Further."

Merlow prayed beneath his breath. *God and the Great Spirit protect ye my love!* As he moved backwards, further away.

Ming nodded and Merlow stopped.

"Stay there," said Ming.

"Let her go!" Merlow's anxiety for Hetty reached a fever pitch, he wanted desperately to break and run towards her, but his training held him still. If he moved, he would put her in more danger.

Ming ignored him and began edging towards the sword and the text with Hetty still clasped to him. Merlow watched with fast beating heart. Whether his prayer had been heard or not, he noticed that Hetty's earlier terror seemed to have transformed into a calm, but tense waiting. She no longer struggled or made a sound. *My brave lass!* He swallowed a sudden lump in his throat.

Ming reached the rock and let Hetty go, giving her a gentle push in Merlow's direction. With a little whimper of relief, she ran towards him. He took two steps towards her, catching her in his arms.

"Hetty!" he hugged her close. "I'm so sorry! Are ye all right love?"

She clung to him, trembling, her face buried in his shirt. "Yes!"

"Leave her and face me!" called Ming. He had unsheathed the sword and stood in bent-kneed fighting stance, with the sword raised.

Merlow shoved Hetty behind him with an urgent, "Run love! Run!"

Hetty shook her head and backed away to stand behind the rock where the text still sat. "I won't leave you," she mouthed at him, her hands clasped tightly together, her expression taut with worry. Heartened by this show of support, even as he worried still for her safety, he sent another prayer to the Great Spirit and one to his Master, for their blessing.

Merlow advanced on Ming, glad that he'd had the foresight to grab the knife, extracting it from his boot. He took up a similar stance to Ming's, breathing out slowly and forcing his mind to focus. He drew on his chi and waited.

The stream of moonlight across the ground gave them enough light to see each other but caused deep shadows and drained everything of colour.

The night was eerily still around them and the air chilly, although he was too hot to feel the cold penetrate his limbs.

Ming shifted and he followed suit, mirroring the other man's moves. They circled each other slowly, and he wondered how he was going to best the man with only a knife against the sacred sword.

Time ticked away as they circled, stretching his nerves to the breaking point. Merlow breathed deeply, reaching for the calm place within that his master had taught him was the well spring of his strength, and continued to wait on the other man to strike first. It was risky. Ming could kill him with one stroke of the sword in the right place. But Merlow had to trust to his instincts to save him from that.

Finally, Ming swung the sword two handed in a circle, and shifting his weight forward, lunged. Merlow danced out of reach and twisted and leapt, to land almost behind the other man and slashed with his knife cutting through the shoulder of Ming's leather coat. A dark upwelling of fluid told him the knife had found flesh.

The fighting became fierce, cutting and parry-ing, violent swings of the sword blocked repeatedly by, to Merlow's surprise, his knife. Near miss after near miss, as he danced out of reach, twisted, turned and leapt to stay the man's increasingly des-perate attempts to slay him.

Merlow was tiring, his arm ached, his breathing laboured, sweat congealing on his skin beneath his shirt. But Ming was tiring too. The man was at least ten years older than he, and despite his training and experience, he was nearing the limits of his strength, Merlow could feel it. *If he could hold on for a little bit longer...*

Ming spun, cutting a swathe with the sword that narrowly missed Merlow's stomach. With a thudding heart, Merlow rolled out of the way, springing to his feet, and made a run at the other man with his knife. *He needed to end this...*

Ming knocked the knife from his hand with the heavy blade of the sword, which jarred Merlow's wrist, and pain and exhaustion sent him to his knees. Ming flung the sword into the air, catching the hilt with both hands. The blade directed towards the earth; he brought it down over the back of Merlow's neck.

"No!" Hetty's shriek cut through the air, as she tore towards them, the text held out in her hands. "Take it! It's what you want, isn't it? Please, don't kill him!"

Ming's trajectory halted, as Hetty flung the text at him, and he dropped the sword to catch it, the thin pages fluttering between their leather binding.

His knees gave way as he did it, and he sank to the earth. Tears starting down his face.

Merlow raised his head, still stunned he hadn't been beheaded. Rising, he caught Hetty against him as she flung herself at him, sobbing.

"Hush love, I'm all right," he murmured, gulping air.

A sound from Ming brought his attention back to the kneeling man, who was clutching his chest, the text fallen to the ground before him.

Ming gasped; his eyes wide. "I am unworthy!" he whispered in mandarin. "The Great Spirit has rejected me!" The agony in his voice and face made Merlow drop to his knees before him.

"He is having an apoplexy!" he said, recognising the symptoms. Ming swayed and Merlow caught him, laying him flat on the ground.

Ming's breath hitched. "I was wrong! You are the blessed one!" he whispered. His neck arched in agony and his body slowly slumped back onto the ground. His eyes staring sightlessly at the heavens.

"Damn, not ye too!" said Merlow in anguish, applying compressions to his chest in a desperate attempt to revive him.

HETTY STOOD WATCHING HELPLESSLY as Merlow worked frantically to revive the Chinese man who had so lately threatened them both. After a good twenty minutes Merlow slumped in defeat.

"He's gone! I cannae bring him back no matter what I do!" He covered his face with his hand and his shoulders shook. She dropped to her knees and put her arms round him.

"It's not your fault! You tried my love," she murmured, wanting desperately to comfort him and relieve his pain.

Merlow took a breath and wiped the tears from his face. "I'm a doctor Hetty, ye ken I'm supposed to save lives, not cause deaths! That's four men who have died because o' me. I didna kill em directly perhaps, but they're dead all the same because of my actions. It doesna sit well with me."

"It's not your fault!" she said fiercely. Refusing to admit he was to blame for any of it. "They chose to come after you. You did nothing more than defend yourself and the items you were sworn to protect. And me!" she added with a little smile through her tears. "I didn't quite believe you would kill for me, but you would, wouldn't you?"

He cupped her face. "Yes, lass I would. For all

my Hippocratic oath, I would for you. You and our bairns, if we're blessed to have any."

"Oh, Merlow!" She flung her arms round his neck and clung to him, her tears soaking the shoulder of his shirt.

He hugged her close and kissed her hair and eventually she raised her face, and he kissed her. His lips warm and soft, his arms comforting. She was where she was meant to be. This man was her fate and destiny, and she was glad now that her teenage fall from grace kept her from marriage until he found her. He was her true soul mate.

Breaking the kiss reluctantly, he said, "I'd best fetch Seb love, I'll need some help with the body. He should be cremated in accordance with his beliefs ye ken?"

She nodded and rose reluctantly to her feet. He rose too and gathered up the sword, sheathing it in its scabbard. She picked up the text and handed it to him, as he slipped his knife in one boot and picking up Ming's knife from the ground where he had dropped it, slid it into his other boot.

They headed back to the house, where he stashed the sword, text and knives away after he had cleaned them.

Straightening, he went to the bowl of water to wash, stripping off his sweaty blood-stained shirt and held it in his hands a moment, staring at the blood. He could not pretend to himself any longer that he wasn't capable of killing. He'd have killed Ming tonight if he'd hurt Hetty. As it was, the man's body had betrayed him. Or was it the Great Spirit? God? Protecting the sacred items entrusted to his care?

His legs gave out suddenly, and he sat abruptly in the chair before the fireplace, his shirt still clutched in his hands, overwhelmed by the implications of that.

Hetty found him still sitting there several minutes later.

She came to him immediately, sensing something was wrong and placed her hands on his shoulders.

"What is it?" she murmured. Digging her fingers into the taut muscles in his shoulders.

"Overwhelm lass. The implications of all this just hit me." He laid the shirt on the arm of the chair, and clasped her hands where they rested on his shoulders, leaning his head against the back of the chair. She leaned over and kissed his forehead.

"You were so brave, so strong, and I was terrified every minute, he was going to kill you!" she confessed. Her voice cracking.

He gave a crack of laughter that broke in middle. "I was too lass, although that was easier to bear than watching him hold a knife to your throat."

She came around the chair and sat in his lap and wrapped his arms round her. They sat like that in silence for a few minutes.

"I don't think I fully realised until now what a sacred trust I'd been given. I don't know why or how, but it would seem the Great Spirit believes me worthy of that trust." He swallowed. "When I went to China, I was a young man looking for a purpose, looking for something to fill the hole in my soul. I found it with Master Zhanghu-Zi. My spiritual father. I shall miss him 'til the day I die." He wiped tears off his cheeks.

She hugged him tight in wordless sympathy, he could feel it and knew he was home at last, for with Hetty he had everything he had ever craved or wanted. *She was the home and hearth he needed.*

Burying his nose in her hair, he held her close and murmured in Gaelic "Is tu solas m' anama agus socrachadh mo chridhe."

"What was that?" asked Hetty raising her head.

"Ye are the light of my soul and hearts ease."

"Oh Merlow! And you are mine!" she whispered.

He kissed her lips softly and said, "I should dress so I can take ye home, before I forget myself and take ye to bed instead."

She got off his lap and he had a quick wash, put on a clean shirt, and a jacket and neckcloth. "Do I look sufficiently respectable to ask ye father to put up the bans, d ye think?" He asked.

She combed his hair off his forehead and kissed him.

"You look very handsome Doctor Thornton. And not at all as if you have just been fighting for our lives. You are my hero." She kissed him again and he hugged her convulsively.

"And ye are my reason for living," he whispered. "I know how Mitch feels. If I lost ye…"

She swallowed and smiled mistily at him. "But you didn't. I feel the same about you, Merlow."

They stood a moment holding each other close, and then clearing his throat, he said, "come I'll take ye home, before yer father sends out a search party. Seb and I'll will attend to Ming later."

She slipped her hand in his arm, and they left

the house to walk up the street to the vicarage in the darkness.

"Hetty!" The vicar appeared from the parlour as they entered the front door. "Where have you been?" He looked from his daughter's flushed face and sparkling eyes to Merlow, his eyebrows rising. "Am I to gather congratulations are in order?"

Merlow slipped his arm round Hetty's waist and gave the vicar a little bow. "They are sir, you'll do me the favour of publishing the banns as soon as possible?"

"I'll be delighted to my dear chap, come in and have a drink. Hetty my dearest girl I could not be more delighted with this news!" The vicar hugged his daughter and pushed them both into the parlour while he went off to find Mrs Corcoran and deliver the good news.

News travels fast in a small village, and not ten minutes later Seb and Bethany burst in upon them in the parlour. As her brother and sister-in-law mobbed Hetty with hugs and kisses and congratulations, the vicar sidled sideways and murmured to Merlow, "I don't know how you did it, but I'm very happy you did."

"Persistence, sir."

"And sincerity of heart. Even a blind man could see you adore my Hetty, I've no qualms you'll care for as she should be cared for."

"Thankye sir, yer right. I'd die for her."

"Well, I hope you won't! That'll do her no good at all!" quipped the vicar, pushing his glasses back up his nose.

"Nay sir I've no intention of leaving her."

"Or us I hope, Pinner has quite come to depend on you."

"I may take her to visit my brother for a wee spell, but that is all."

Managing to nab a quiet word with Seb he gave him the bare bones of the situation and requested his help with Ming's body and Seb agreed to meet him in the spinney at midnight.

It was another hour before Merlow could drag himself away from Hetty and her family. She came to the door to see him off with a kiss and a whispered *I love you* that set his heart singing.

He returned home to change and meet Seb in the spinney.

Seb didn't turn a hair at the sight of the body or the blood. He lifted Ming easily and carried him back to Merlow's compounding room, where he laid him on the table and helped Merlow strip and wash and prepare the body. Once done, he helped him take the body back out to the forest where they made a funeral pyre and laid the body on it.

Setting fire to it, Merlow made an offering and some prayers for the release of Ming's spirit, while Seb watched on in silence. They stood watch over the pyre together, until it burned to ash, as the sky began to lighten, heralding the start of a new day.

"Thank you," said Merlow, offering a charcoal covered hand.

Seb smiled a small smile and shook his head. "No thanks needed, brother."

Merlow blinked his eyes at the address. Strange how he could feel so accepted and loved by these strangers, when his own flesh and blood had rejected him so thoroughly. He had thought that rejection had ceased to hurt, seems he was wrong. He knew Col loved him in his way, but he didn't understand him. He never would; they were too different.

His conscience in regard to Col bothered him. He really should go back to see him; he had left so abruptly. He would take Hetty to meet him. It was the least he could do.

Seb gathered up the implements they had used and said quietly, "it's not the first body I've disposed of, though I hope it will be the last. I'd thought to put all that behind me."

Merlow swallowed and wiped his face wearily with a grubby handkerchief. He'd gathered from the little that Seb had let fall, the man wasn't a chatterbox, that his former role working for Mr Lovell in London had involved some unsavoury tasks.

"Well, I appreciate the assistance and I give you my word, Hetty will not suffer because of her association with me. This should be the end of it. I doubt there are any more Chinese men lurking about trying to kill me."

"I hope not," rumbled Seb.

CHAPTER 19

*M*erlow waited nervously at the altar with his soon to be brother-in-law. As he'd promised Hetty he was wearing his kilt and a new jacket for the occasion. "Do ye have the ring?" he asked turning to Seb.

"Aye," said Seb with his usually relaxed rumble. The big man clapped him on the shoulder and squeezed. "That's the third time you've asked. Relax."

Merlow flushed, it wasn't like him to be so agitated, he was forgetting all his training. He took a breath and reached for the calm place inside him. A few breaths later he opened his eyes at a nudge from Seb and turned as the noise in the church suddenly subsided.

At the entrance to the small church, Hetty, gowned in pale green silk with pink roses stood with her father. At sight of her, his heart lifted, and he smiled. His lass was beautiful and very soon she would be his to love, cherish and protect for the rest of his life.

The organist struck up a piece from Handel, and Hetty and Mr Rooke senior began to make their way down the aisle towards him. When they reached him, Mr Rooke took her hand and placed it in Merlow's with a murmured, "she's your responsibility now." Then he stepped up into the raised dais before the altar and took his place behind the lectern.

"Dear parishioners of Pinner," he began, "we are gathered today for a very special and joyous occasion, one I have personally looked forward to for a long time. The marriage of my precious daughter, Henrietta Louise Rooke to Merlow Douglas Thornton." He paused a moment to clear his throat and Merlow looked sideways at Hetty and squeezed her hand as she smiled and blinked rapidly.

"You all know these two very well I think, and you will agree with me that they are a match blessed by God, for no two people have brought more happiness to this parish than the pair of them, singly and together. I am justly proud of my Hetty and equally proud to welcome Merlow to our family, for no man could be more deserving of my precious girl than him."

The vicar stopped to blow his nose and Merlow was conscious of both his own flushed countenance and the warmth in his breast at such a compliment from his father-in-law. Behind him there were sighs and muffled sobs, from several quarters. A surreptitious look revealed the Misses Fielding who were sat in the front pew, Amelia crying openly, while Doris sniffed and surreptitiously blew her nose.

As Merlow made his vows to love, honour and protect, his heart swelled with joy and love, and his cup spilled over when Hetty, holding his hands tightly in hers, looked up at him and made hers to love, honour and obey with her whole heart in her eyes.

"I love ye Hetty," he murmured between his vows, as he slid his ring on her finger.

"I love you Merlow," she responded softly, between promising to remain faithful in sickness and in health.

When they left the church, the O'Donnell children formed a guard of honour for them as they were showered with rose petals and well wishes from the crowd.

Mrs O'Donnell, who told her husband roundly that she wasn't missing this wedding for the world, had been carried to the church in an old-fashioned carrying chair, by her four eldest sons, and from there to the Bulls Head where the wedding celebrations were being hosted by Beth and Seb.

Mitch Stewart attended the wedding with Mrs Craig, who seemed to have taken her duties to keep an eye on him to heart.

Mrs Carson sat with her son and daughter-in-law, Sarah Wakelin's sister, and their brood of five and beamed happily at the bride and groom.

HETTY HUGGED HER FATHER, "thank you for those lovely words you said about me and Merlow" she said. "You almost had me in tears."

"Truer words never spoken my dear, I am so

proud of you. Couldn't be happier to see you wed to Merlow."

"Thank you, Papa!" She hugged him again. He was putting on weight at last, and seemed to be recovering from his illness.

She turned to take wishes and gifts from their guests who seemed determined to drown the happy couple in largess. She had more pots of jam, doilies and lace aprons than she knew what to do with.

It was quite some time before they could settle to the meal Beth had lovingly prepared. That sweet girl had slaved for hours to prepare the wedding breakfast, Hetty was sure. When she got a chance, she hugged Beth and thanked her.

"My absolute pleasure Hetty!" Bethy said with a big smile. "I love cooking, you know I do!"

"I do know, you've out done yourself!" Hetty said.

"I'm so happy for you," Beth said. "Merlow is lovely."

"Yes, he is," said Hetty with a besotted smile in her husband's direction. He was talking to the Misses Fielding, bless him. He was so patient and kind. Her heart was full.

IT WAS late afternoon before the bride and groom were able to escape their well-wishers and the groom was able to carry his bride over the threshold of her new home and shut the door on the world.

"Well Mrs Thornton," he said, resting his hands on her waist. "Are ye happy with yer new abode?"

"I am Mr Thornton," she said with a warm smile, cupping his face with her hands. "But I do have plans for some refurbishments, if you've no objection."

"None love, do what ye will with the place, I'm just over the moon to have ye to myself at last. That's what comes of marrying the most popular lass in the village I suppose."

She leaned up and kissed him and a few minutes later he said breathless and low, "Upstairs Hetty?"

She nodded, "yes please Merlow."

Scooping her up he carried her up the stairs to his bedchamber where between heated kisses they tore off each other's clothes with more haste than care. "At last!" he groaned pulling her naked body against his. Scooping her up he deposited her gently on the bed and took a moment to appreciate her.

"Yer beautiful Hetty," he murmured kneeling on the bed as she blushed under his scrutiny, her hands going to cover herself. "Don't hide from me sweetheart," he bent and kissed her lips, her throat her breasts. "I've longed for this my darling, we shall go as slow as you like, and as I promised ye, it shall not hurt."

She reached up and pulled him closer, a hand running over his chest. "I know, I'm not afraid anymore, I want this as much as you do."

"I doubt that love," he said with a husky laugh, "but I'm glad to know you feel that way." His hand stroked down her body, glorying in the beauty of her soft skin and curves. Cupping each breast again and suckling them in turn he listened to her in drawn breath, the little sounds of her pleasure and stroked lower with his other hand seeking the entrance to her body with his fingers. Eager to feel the evidence of her arousal, how much she wanted him, on his fingers.

"Ah yer so we love!" he said husky voiced.

He reached for the little bottle on the bedside table and poured a few drops onto his fingers. Swirling it round the entrance to her body he added more to his fingers and pushed them inside her, adding some more as he pushed deeper, rousing her with his thumb in the way he knew she liked. He added a third finger to stretch her, looking for signs of discomfort, she seemed to evince none, on the contrary pushing up into his strokes, whimpering and gasping.

With hands well coated in neem oil he stroked his cock which was straining at the prospect before him. He tamped down his desire as best he could, his focus on Hetty and what would feel good for her. He was aware that he was being a bit clinical about this, rather than letting the passion flow naturally, perhaps that was a mistake, but he was wary of losing control, which he thought he might. He wanted her fiercely, and he didn't wish to scare her.

"Ye feel ready to me love, are ye?" he asked putting the neem oil aside and positioning himself between her legs.

She nodded, "I think so."

"Lift yer legs a bit higher," he suggested. She obeyed and he lined his cock up, notching the head to the entrance of her body, his pulse beating heavy in his throat, thrills of desire radiating outwards from the touch of her most intimate place to his.

"Ready?" he asked again, more nervous than his teenaged-self had been the first time he breached a woman's body.

She smiled and nodded, "Yes, please Merlow."

With a deep breath he pushed forward and was engulfed in tight heat, the pleasure of it stopped his breath and he groaned involuntarily, his eyes closing in reflex. Forcing them open he stared down at her anxiously, "All right?"

"Yes, it feels full, like I'm stretched, but it doesn't hurt."

"Good," some of his anxiety dropped away. He began to move slowly at first, his hand reaching between them to provide the extra stimulus she would need, watching her face for reactions. Ignoring the promptings of his own body to push harder and faster, he moved steadily, building her slowly, he hoped, towards release. He began to worry that he should have brought her to crisis before commencing coitus, especially as time drew out, and it was obvious she wasn't any closer.

"What is it love, do want me to stop?" he asked.

"N-no. It feels as if you're staring at me, as if you're worried about something."

He closed his eyes. "Sorry. Aye I am. I'm over-thinking this. I'm so concerned for you to feel good I'm ruining it." He lowered his head to the pillow beside hers, and she reached up to stroke his hair.

"Just kiss me, Merlow," she said softly. "Make me feel like you love me."

"I do love ye, so much I'm tying myself in knots. Yer a wise woman Hetty," he murmured, moving sideways and disengaging their bodies, pulling her close, with them both on their sides facing each other, he kissed her. His hands stroking her back and hip, bringing her leg over his, he cradled her buttock in one hand while he deepened the kiss. Feeling her respond, pressing her breasts against his chest.

His other arm, the one beneath her, wrapped round her tight, and he moved the hand under her buttock, forward, dragging his fingers lightly through her wet flesh, stroking and pushing his fingers inside her.

She moved against him, rubbing her nipples on his chest, her body undulating against him, her breath catching as she made noises in her throat. *Yes! Aye Yes!*

His cock pulsed against the inside of her thigh, butting up against his hand as he worked his fingers inside her, and the ache of desire he'd been trying to suppress burst through with over-whelming force. He deepened the kiss, plundering her mouth with the passion he'd been trying to keep at bay, feeling his control slipping away in the wake of her increasingly frenzied response.

His hips wouldn't keep still, pushing his cock up against his hand even as he worked her body deeper with four fingers, his breathing hoarse and ragged in her ear as he held her tight. Withdrawing his hand abruptly, he poked and prodded blindly with his cock until he found the right place and pushed into her body with a hard thrust. His hand locking onto her hip as he stroked deep and firm.

She gasped and squirmed on him, meeting each deep thrust with a curl of her hips. His hand squeezed her buttock hard as he pushed deeper, faster, his breathing going ragged. "Hetty! Hetty love!" he groaned, hoping she was with him, but unable to stop the drive towards completion, now that he was here. It felt so damned good, his whole body was suffused with tingling pleasure and the epicentre of it, where their bodies joined, became for a few moments his whole existence.

She writhed in his grip and panted, moaning with him, and he felt the moment her body stiffened with a whimpering moan just as his body tipped over the edge in an explosion of pleasure that stopped thought, breath and time. Shuddering with the force of the electric release, he hung onto her through the waves of it like he'd been flung down rapids and was in danger of drowning if he let her go.

As he gave up his seed in hot jets of exquisite release, he groaned repeatedly, the pulsing spasms wringing the last of the pleasure from his body and leaving him limp and floating in its wake.

Coming to his senses slowly, he opened his eyes to find Hetty's head close to his own on the pillow, her eyes were closed, her expression he could only describe as sated, which made him smile with satisfaction.

"Sweetheart," he murmured kissing her gently. She stirred in his arms and opened her eyes.

"Hmm," she murmured and nuzzled her face against his beard. He smiled and pulled her close. They were still joined, and he didn't want to disengage yet, this aftermath was raw and sweet and wonderful.

"Yer truly my wife now love," he said against

her ear, and she nuzzled closer with a mumbled murmur that might have been *I love you.*

After a bit he finally withdrew and fetched a cloth to tidy her up before climbing back into bed and settling her with her head on his chest and a leg straddling his thighs. This, he thought, was what he had waited all his life for.

HETTY NUZZLED INTO MERLOW, she couldn't get enough of his fur! She sighed in contentment. All those years of lonely anguish faded as if they were a bad dream. She was glad now that she had steadfastly refused every previous offer made to her, for if she hadn't, she would have been married to someone else when Merlow came to Pinner and that would have been a tragedy. He was her perfect man, her perfect match. She loved him so much her heart couldn't contain it.

Thank you, Lord, she prayed silently. *Thank you for sending him to me. I didn't think I deserved happiness, but I have been proven wrong. I will try very hard to be worthy of this precious gift of love.*

EPILOGUE

*H*etty's first sight of Merlow's home was in the light of the dying sun as their horses took them down the driveway towards the double-fronted, two-story, grey stone building. They had ridden in easy stages from Pinner, taking over a week to get here. The doctor from Harrow would pick up Merlow's patients for the duration of their trip, they planned to be away for a month.

"The stables are round this way," said Merlow leading the way to the left side of the house.

The stables were stone and thatch, with a couple of nags in the stalls and a freckle faced, tow-headed boy sitting in the sun on a stump whittling at a piece of wood.

"Willy!" greeted Merlow dismounting from his horse.

The lad looked up and grinned and the next exchange was conducted entirely in Gaelic. Merlow had been teaching her a few phrases, but this exchange was too rapid and with too strong an accent for her to catch any of it.

Merlow helped her down from her horse and introduced her, as the boy came forward to take the horses.

"Hetty this is Willy, Fergus's grandson. Fergus is my brother's umm, butler, cook and steward I suppose. Willy looks after the stables. He grew up here with my nephews, Callum and Rory. He doesna speak much English I'm afraid."

"Willy, this is my wife. Bhean. Ye ken?"

Willy nodded and tugged his forelock with a shy smile.

"Where's Fergus?" Merlow asked.

"Master Merlow!" A small, wizened man appeared round the corner of the house, with grey hair and untidy beard, dressed in worn breeches and leather jerkin he carried a rifle in one hand and sack in the other.

"Fergus! Been hunting, I see," said Merlow with a smile.

"Aye coineanaich," said Fergus lifting the sack.

"We'll be getting rabbit stew for dinner," translated Merlow.

Hetty tried to hide her flinch and smiled as Merlow made the introductions. Fergus seemed to have more English than his grandson and accompanied them into the house, Willy trailing with their luggage.

The house was dim inside with wood panelling and dark heavy furniture. A number of heavily antlered deer's heads glared at them from the walls, and she sidled instinctively closer to Merlow as he led her towards the stairs, just as two boys yelling at the tops of their voices hurtled down them at breakneck speed.

"Callum, Rory!" Merlow's bellow brought the boys to a halt halfway down the stairs.

"Uncail!" Rory the taller of the two with darker hair, came down the remaining stairs with a slight swagger. "Himself thought ye'd abandoned us!"

"What the bluidy hell is all this racket?" A big red-headed man emerged from a room beside the stairs.

"Speak of the devil!" muttered Callum with a twist of his mouth.

"Merlow!" the man snorted. "Decided to come back did ye?"

"Aye grumble shanks!" responded Merlow moving towards him. "I brought my wife to meet ye!" He hugged his brother; the resemblance was strong enough for there to be no mistaking the relationship. And turned to wave Hetty forward.

"Hetty this is Col, my older brother and the Laird Sceanchain."

"My Lord," said Hetty politely, dropping a curtsy.

"Good God! Ye left to go to a bluidy symposium and ye come back married to a Sassenach! The old man I'd turn in his grave, if he weren't already roasting in hell!"

"Damn it Col!" muttered Merlow flushing.

Col eyed Hetty, and finally cracked a smile. It changed his whole face, lighting it up and making it look a great deal younger, and handsomer. "Forgive me manners my dear, we don't get women in the house very often." He took her hand and kissed it with old-fashioned courtesy. "Welcome to Sceanchain House, such as it is." He turned to Merlow. "How long you planning to stay this time?"

"Two weeks. I've set up practice in Pinner, which is where I met Hetty, she's the vicar's daughter. I've patients waiting for me to return. I'm sorry Col, but we'll come to visit more frequently I promise. You could always come and see us."

"Hmm." Col snorted. "Fergus are any of the rooms fit to house a lady?"

"Not yet, but give me an hour mi Lord and I'll have the yellow suite made up. You two," he addressed the boys, "can help restuff the mattress."

"Good notion," Col threw a look at his son's that dared them to defy this order. For a moment Hetty thought Rory would, the fulminating look of fury and contempt he gave his father made her gasp. But with a shrug he turned and tromped back up the stairs followed by his younger brother.

"I'll just dump these, and I'll be up," said Fergus wandering off to a back part of the house where Hetty surmised the kitchens were.

"I can help," she called after him and went to follow. Merlow stayed her with a hand on her arm.

"Yer a guest Hetty yer not expected to work."

"I can't sit idle when there is work to be done, you know that Merlow."

"Aye I do. Well, if ye must, but don't go lifting anything heavy."

"I won't," she smiled and kissed his cheek before going after Fergus.

She followed him through a door in the back wall of the hall which lead through to the mud room and rear entrance to the house and the kitchens off to the left.

Fergus had dumped a brace of rabbits on the

large wooden table and was decanting hot water from a large pot on the fire into a pail.

"What can I do to help?" she asked looking about. The kitchen at least was clean.

Fergus blinked at her. "Nay lass, there's naught to do."

"Nonsense. Do you have flour and eggs and other staples?"

"Aye..." he said slowly.

"Good then I shall cook." she glanced at the rabbits and away. "It is beyond me to skin those, but if you do that for me, I can make the stew and a pudding for dinner. Those boys take a fair bit of feeding I don't doubt."

"Aye they do." Then. "The pantry's through there."

She nodded decisively and headed to the pantry.

"WELL, that's a start, getting married. Did ye plan to get wed when ye left here?" asked Col pouring whisky into two glasses.

"Nay, I'd no notion of it." said Merlow taking up the glass. "But I found myself in Pinner, it's a small village just outside of London, attached to Harrow, ye might have heard of that? The school for gentlemen is housed there."

"Aye I've heard of Harrow. But how did ye come to stay there?"

"I met Hetty," he said simply. "I knew the minute I clapped eyes on her."

Col watched him over his glass, his blue eyes going cloudy. "Like that was it?"

"Aye. Took me a while to convince her mind. But it was a case with me the moment I saw her."

Col nodded and sat down in the chair by the fire with sigh. "Like me with Catriona." His gaze landed on the flames and his melancholy expression told Merlow that his brother was still mourning his wife. He looked up at the portrait of her over the fireplace and sighed quietly.

"I'm sorry Col, I've a better notion of what ye've suffered now. The notion of losing Hetty-" he shook his head. "It doesn't bear thinking of."

"Hmm." Col moved uncomfortably in his seat and with an effort he said, "well I'm glad for ye. I hope ye have many years of happiness."

"I plan to," said Merlow, sipping his whisky. He contemplated telling his brother about the Chinese but decided against it. The episode was behind him now and Col would never understand.

Later that evening, after a substantial dinner provided by Hetty's efforts, much to the approbation of his nephews, Merlow crawled into bed with his wife, the freshly stuffed mattress rustling beneath his weight, pulled her close with a sigh and said, "I apologise for my relations, I know they're a little rough round the edges."

"It's all right. They're lonely men. This house needs a woman."

"I know, but it's no likely to happen. I doubt Col is ever going to get over losing Catriona."

"He could employ a housekeeper."

"Nay, I think he prefers it this way."

"Perhaps after a fortnight of female comforts, he might think differently?"

"Perhaps," Merlow nuzzled her neck. "Are ye

too tired love?" he asked tracing kisses down her neck.

"No," she said slightly breathless, rolling to face him.

"Good," he murmured kissing her.

WREN ST CLAIRE

White Lotus
Book 2

The Scottish Laird

Steamy Regency Romance

ABOUT THE SCOTTISH LAIRD

The Scottish Laird Book 2 of the White Lotus Series Steamy Regency Romance

Mulan meets Highlander in this grumpy sunshine romance between a Scottish single dad and a Chinese martial arts master.

Malcolm Douglas Thornton the Laird Mac Sceachain, single father of two wild boys, is still deeply mourning the loss of his wife and daughter from six years ago and the last thing he wants is for his all-male domain to be invaded by a woman.

Ming Aihan, sister of Ming Liang, a trained marital artist and devotee of the Baguadao religion of the White Lotus, is determined to discover what has happened to her older brother and the only name she has is that of the Laird Mac Sceachain.

Cultures clash when these two meet and they struggle to make themselves understood to each other. As barriers of communication slowly fall, a rising attraction turns these enemies to lovers. But even Col's passion for her will not turn Aihan from her mission to avenge the death of her brother and his men.

The White Lotus Series: Where Scottish and Chinese cultures clash, with some unexpected results...

Series reading Order:
Book 1: The Scottish Doctor: Merlow and Hetty
Book 2: The Scottish Laird: Col and Aihan
Book 3: The Scottish Lass: Isa and Caishen

EXCERPT FROM THE SCOTTISH LAIRD

Chapter 1

Aihan stumbled out of her cabin, clutching the walls for balance, the ship was listing dangerously, buffeted by the wind and the waves. She fought her way to the ladder that led onto the deck. Rain lashed her face as soon as she pushed the hatch up, the wind snatched it from her hand and blew it back on the deck with a slam. Scrambling out onto the deck she fought to push it back into place and latch it down.

Around her, the crew scuttled about, tying things down and three of them were wholly occupied in holding the rudder in an attempt to keep the junk from running aground, the anchor seemed to have slipped its mooring and the vessel was heading for the rocks. Their shouts barely registered above the howling wind and the visibility was very poor, the clouds being so heavy and low, the sun was completely obscured.

She clung to the railing, entirely drenched, her

silk tunic and pants clinging to her thin frame indecently, her long dark hair plastered to her face. *Where was Caishen?* She looked about for her brother's student, but couldn't see him. It had been several weeks now since Liang left the ship and there had been no word from him. The anxiety chewing at her was close to boiling point, then the storm had come up out of nowhere this afternoon. It was almost worse than some of the storms they had endured on the voyage from Canton.

"Caishen?" she called, but the wind snatched her voice away.

A loud crack rent the air and for a moment everything was bright as midday. In that second, she saw him clinging to the rigging and swaying in the wind. In the next moment he seemed to lose his grip and his body was falling. She screamed, racing towards the spot as his body plummeted into the water and disappeared from view in the choppy waves.

"Caishen! Help him!" she yelled at the crew who stood near her staring at the place he had disappeared. They backed away making the sign to ward off evil and went back to their work.

The ship listed at that moment, flinging her sideways as a wave breached the deck, drenching her in cold, salty water. Coughing she fought her way over to one of the coiled ropes and staggering towards the rail, fighting to maintain her balance, she tied one end to the rail and the other around her waist. Climbing precariously over the rail, she jumped into the turbulent water and went under.

The cold almost robbed her of breath, and she

surfaced coughing and shuddering as the icy waters seeped into her bones. She turned around, looking for any sign of Caishen, but there was nothing. She struck out swimming, but the waves buffeted her so badly she made little head way and as she had completely lost her bearings, she was soon going round in circles, her limbs beginning to go numb with the cold.

Realising it was a fruitless endeavour, and she would drown if she didn't get back to the ship, she fought her way back to the Shaolin and dragged herself up the side by the hooks. The crew made no move to help her as she heaved herself over the side onto the deck, collapsing with a splash, the heavy sodden rope dragging at her waist.

She sprawled on the deck panting for several moments, eventually with numb fingers she wrestled to unknot the rope and release it from her waist. All the while, the storm continued to rage around the ship, making it roll and heave and rattle, the wind a constant howling, the rain almost horizontal, sheeting water across the deck.

Free of the rope, she clambered to her feet and staggered towards the hatch, fumbling with the latch, her fingers so stiff with cold they almost refused to work, she got it open eventually. Her limbs were shaking so much she couldn't control them. Pulling the hatch back down over her head, she latched it from the inside and battled her way back to her cabin, where she stripped off her sodden garments and dried herself off as best she could.

Wrapping herself in a dry blanket, she crawled

into her bed, pulled the covers over her head and huddled into a shaking ball in an attempt to get warm. *Caishen was gone and Liang was gone.* There was just her and a crew that only wanted to go home. *What was she going to do?* Tears stung her eyes, but she refused to let then fall. That was weakness and Liang had taught her not to be weak.

The storm blew itself out overnight and Aihan emerged from her cabin with a plan. In the daylight the sea was calm, almost flat and the ship was anchored once more, but this time it was nearer to the shore of the land called Scot-land. The strange name was awkward to pronounce.

As the current had brought the ship here to this harbour, perhaps it had also brought Caishen's body? She needed to find out.

She turned to the Captain, Zhou Sheng, he and his men had grown increasingly truculent the longer her brother was gone and had made no secret of their desire to return home. "I am going ashore to look for Caishen's body," she said with decisive authority. If she showed any weakness, she would be lost. There was one of her, and six of them.

"That is madness. We should go home. Master Ming is lost, Shen Caishen is lost. The Gods are telling us to go home!"

She shook her head, "I must find Caishen's body and my brother. Come with me. We will find them together and then go home."

The Captain looked around at his men who were all looking at the deck or the horizon, anywhere but at her.

The Captain shook his head. "I will give you one day."

"Three! Three days," she bargained.

"Very well for Master Ming's sake. Three days, if you are not back by then we will leave for Canton."

She nodded. "Row me to shore in the lifeboat?" They'd had three, but there was only one left. However, the one Liang had taken, or perhaps the one his men who had gone before him had taken, should still be there, and she could use one of them to get back to the ship.

The Captain nodded.

She went below to pack a small backpack, her weapons, cloak and take the last of the strange coins that Liang had gotten in trade before they left Canton. These he had explained to her would give them currency in this peculiar foreign land. He had left her a dozen of them. She had no idea of their value.

Returning to the deck dressed in a fresh tunic and pants, boots upon her feet, cloak wrapped round her shoulders and the pack secured to her breast, she followed the first mate over the rail and down to the rowboat bobbing in the water.

He said nothing to her the whole way, wouldn't even look at her. That hurt. Climbing out of the boat on the shore, she said firmly "I will return in three days. Do not leave without me!"

He nodded and set the oars to row back to the Shaolin. A shiver passed over her skin as a premonition washed through her that she would never see him or the Shaolin and its crew again.

She shook it off, straightened her shoulders and

turned to survey the view before her. Several foreign boats bobbed at anchor in this little harbour and beyond the harbour, trees blanketed the coast to the right, but ahead of her lay buildings and to the left a stretch of beach and tangled rocks and a low escarpment with scrub and wood above it.

She headed to the right first, looking for signs of Caishen's body washed up by the tide, along with seaweed, shells and dead wood. She walked for an hour and found nothing and no sign of the row boats either. Turning back, she retraced her steps, pausing occasionally to sip on her meagre water supply. The sun was warm on her back, although a breeze tugged at her garments and hair as she trudged.

Reaching her starting point, she set off to the left. This took longer because the terrain was more broken up by rocks and there were more places that a body might be wedged, but again after two hours, by the position of the sun, she had found nothing. She returned to the little harbour, her heart heavy. No sign of Caishen, she must conclude the water had taken him or beached him farther afield than she expected. And no sign of the row boats. But perhaps she could hire one to take her back out, if she found some trace of her brother...

This time she struck out for the buildings, conscious that she only had three days to find out what happened to her brother before the ship would sail without her.

Chapter 2

Malcolm Douglas Thornton, the Laird Mac

Sceanchain, and Col to a few intimates, stuck a fork in the piece of mutton on his plate and wrestled his knife through the tough sinews. The fire behind him crackled in the hearth and the clock ticked on the mantelpiece, the only sounds other than those of his dinner companion's knives wrestling with the meat. He sat at the head of the table as befitted the head of the house and his sons dark haired Rory twelve and ginger Callum ten, flanked him. Beyond them sat his elderly servant Fergus and Fergus's grandson Willy, a freckled ginger like Callum, but darker. Such was the extent of his household.

The blessed silence suited his mood, the melancholy had been bad since his brother Merlow had left with his new wife, Hetty, after a fleeting visit of but a fortnight. Hetty's presence, as wonderful as it had been, had stirred up all kinds of memories and Col found himself plunged once more into the kind of dark fog he had not experienced for a year or more.

To have a pretty woman in the kitchen cooking delicious meals, cleaning the layers of dust off the furniture, putting flowers in vases and singing– singing! Col shook his head to shake off the memory, it hurt too much.

And to see his brother's happiness– not that he begrudged it to him. Merlow had waited a long time to take a wife, and he had chosen well. The lass was perfect for him, a vicar's daughter, full of good works and hardworking spirit, the love between the newly-wed's was palpable. And her presence had cut up all Col's hard-won peace.

He had thought himself accustomed to his widowhood, resigned to this lonely state before she came. After she left, he realised all over again, what he had lost with Catriona's death.

"Ow!" exclaimed Callum jerking in his seat and glaring across the table at his grinning elder brother. "What was that for?"

"I was aiming for the dog and your knee must have got in the way," said Rory chewing on his bone.

"Ye'll nae kick the dogs!" roared Col, slamming his fist on the table and making everything jump.

Rory turned a sullen face towards him. "It was a joke Papa, of course I wouldn't kick the dogs."

"But it's alright to kick me!" muttered Callum.

"Nae tis not alright to kick ye," replied Col. "Ye'l apologise to yer brother," he addressed Rory.

Rory pursed his lips and remained silent.

"I said," repeated Col, dangerously slow. "Ye'll apologise to yer brother."

Rory rose and threw his napkin on the table, turning to walk away.

Col shot out a hand and grabbed his arm yanking him back around. "Ye'll do as I say boy or get yer breeches clouted!"

Rory stood silently seething, his fists clenched by his sides. "It was an accident I swung my legs too far out, tis all! I didnae mean to kick him!"

"Tell it to him, not me!"

Rory turned his head and addressed his brother sulkily. "I'm sorry ye little winger! I didnae mean to hurt ye! Yer such a puling little thing, always crying aboot somethin'!"

"Now sit down and finish yer meal!" Col yanked him back into his seat. Rory resumed eating and Col glowered at both boys over his pot of ale. Callum sniffed into his plate.

Col knew from experience this wouldn't be the end of it. Callum wouldn't be able to resist retaliating in some way.

The sequel came quicker than he expected. He'd withdrawn with his dogs, Hector the terrier and Gussie the deerhound, to his study, with a glass of whisky, when a blood-curdling howl brought him out into the hallway.

"I'll kill ye, yer little gobshite!" bellowed Rory appearing at the top of the stairs, something clutched in his hands. "Ye've ruined me buckler! Ye fecking little worm!" He dropped the buckler and took off after a cackling Callum down the hall. A shout and slammed door told Col that Callum had made it to sanctuary and locked the door in his brother's face. As Rory pounded on the door and shouted insults through it, Col climbed the stairs to deal with this latest chapter in the war between his sons. It had erupted following Hetty and Merlow's departure and had been raging now for two weeks with no signs of abating. It seemed he wasn't the only one impacted by Hetty's absence.

Reaching the top of the stairs he strode down the corridor and seized his eldest son by the collar and shook him. "Enough! I'll deal with this, go to yer room and stay there!"

"But he-" began Rory red-faced and puffing.

"I said I'd deal with it. Now get!"

Rory threw him a venomous look and turned away muttering.

"What was that?"

Rory stopped, his shoulders hunching. "Nothing sir."

Col yanked him round. "Say yer piece!"

Rory's fists clenched and he let fly, "ye always favour him, and he's such a weakling! It's nae fair! Grandpa would've flogged him for half the things he's done!"

"If ye didnae bait him in the first place he wouldnae retaliate! Ye bring it on yerself boy! Yer bigger and stronger than him and ye know it. But he's the one with wits, use your heid a bit more boy and ye won't find yerself in so many scraps!"

"Grandpa-"

"Yer Granfather's dead boy and yer stuck with me! Not yer preference I know, but I'm Laird now and ye'll do as I say, now go to bed before I clout ye round the heid for disobedience!"

Rory brought his fists up. "Go on then!"

Col looked down at him and suppressed the urge to laugh, a faint wisp of pride surging through his chest. Rory was a brave lad. Foolish but brave. If he didn't infuriate him so much...

Col scooped the boy up under his arm and marched him down the hall while Rory yelled at him and rained wild punches with his fists against his stomach and chest. Opening the boy's bedroom door he dropped his eldest son onto his bed and shut the door, turning the lock. "Stay there 'till yer heid's cool!"

"Argh!" followed by some thumps of things being thrown at the door followed him down the hall to the other door where his other son cowered. On the way, he stopped to pick up the dropped buckler and examine the damage.

A deep gouge across the Sceanchain escutcheon, featuring a bear rampant, bore mute witness to Callum's spite. The buckler was a family heirloom dating to at least the 16th Century and probably earlier. His father had gifted it to Rory as the eldest son and heir. His father had made no secret of his favouritism towards Rory over Callum, an echo of his preference for Col over his brother Merlow as they grew up. That preference had driven Merlow from his home and caused him to be absent when their father died.

A sudden fury with his father seized Col at this evidence of the damage his favoritism wrought even beyond the grave. He himself was hard on Rory as his father had been on him, but tried where he could, to temper his natural toughness with his younger son, having seen what happens when a father rejects a more sensitive boy. Merlow had simply left home and never come back until after his father was gone.

But staring at the spiteful damage to a family heirloom made it difficult to be sympathetic towards Callum in this instance. Tightly reigning in his anger, he stopped outside Callum's door.

"Callum!"

Silence.

"Callum, open the bluidy door or ye'll regret it!"

After a moment he heard the lock being turned, but the door still didn't open. He pushed the door open himself and stepped into the room. Unlike Rory's room, which was a mess, Callum's was neat as a pin.

Callum sat on his bed staring at the floor.

Col shut the door behind him and leaned

against it, the buckler clutched in one hand, his arms crossed over his chest. His heart thudded heavily in his chest and he felt slightly sick. After a moment or two of silence he prompted, "Well, what ye got to say fer yerself?"

Callum shrugged and kept his head down.

"I should belt the living daylights out of ye for this Callum. This is a bluidy heirloom! Have ye no respect for the family name?"

Callum shrugged again and something in Col snapped. Dropping the buckler, he strode across the room and hauled the boy up by his collar and shook him.

"If ye've none ,I'll teach it to ye!" he growled. "How dare ye take yer petty spite out on something that matters so much, not just to yer brother but the whole family! Generations past and future. There is no balance in yer revenge boy! Rory's crime doesnae match your vengeance, not even close!"

Callum hung his head but said nothing beyond a faint whimper.

"Drop yer breeches boy! Ye'll no sit down for a week! And think yerself lucky to escape with no more than a flogging."

He removed his belt as Callum let his breeches fall and bent over the bed.

Col left his son weeping into his pillow, his bottom red raw from the strapping. He unlocked Rory's door, but there was no sound from within, and he left the boy alone, taking the buckler downstairs with him, he sat it on the table beside his chair and resumed his glass of whisky, staring at the design on the buckler until his eyes blurred. Gussie lay at his feet and Hector leaped into his lap and settled.

He finished the glass and poured another from the decanter.

The morning light found him still in the chair, the fire burned down and the decanter empty. His head was pounding and his bladder full.

With a groan he moved, dislodging Hector who leaped down to the rug and stretched with a squeaking yawn. Gussie sat up and thumped her tail, floppy ears flapping.

He blinked blearily at them and muttered, "Fook me heid's like to split."

Rising he staggered towards the door and out into the hall towards the kitchen and the rear entrance to the house. Emerging into the glare of the early morning, he squinted and headed towards the pump where he dunked his head in the trough and drank some fresh water from the pump with his hands. Straightening he stretched his creaking back and filled a bowl with water for Hector, Gussie was tall enough to drink from the trough.

Hector drank and then cocked his leg against the trough.

"Good idea mate," murmured Col and moved over to a bush, opened his breeches and relieved his bladder.

It was a fine morning, slightly misty and judging from the position of the sun, still quite early. The dogs frisked about, and he said, "alright, we'll go fer a walk, shall we? Blow the cobwebs out."

He left the courtyard behind the house, setting off across the lawn towards the trees. The dogs gambolled about chasing smells, and he lengthened his stride, wanting to get the blood flowing, his thoughts on last night. He needed to do something about the boys, but he was at a loss to know what. He was reaping the consequences of his own neglect of them following Catriona's death. He'd been so grief stricken with the loss of her and their third child, a girl, he'd lost sight of what was important.

He'd dragged himself out of that pit of despond eventually, but by then the damage was done. What frightened him now was the fear that he was about to slip back into that place again. It had been over six years since Cat was taken from him. He was resigned to being alone for the rest of his life, but it was unfair to his boys to let his misery dictate their lives as well. Callum's actions last night had shocked him to the core.

The dogs had wandered off, and he was so sunk in gloom he didn't register anything until the blow between the shoulder blades sent him stumbling forward onto his knees.

A cry of "Aiyee!" behind him was all the warning he got before he was knocked flat on his face by another blow and something heavy landing on his back. If he'd been less hungover and more awake, his reactions would have been quicker. As it was, he lay stunned with the breath knocked out of him for a moment before he heaved sideways throwing off the person who had landed on him and discovered his assailant was female.

At least he thought she was a female, but she was the strangest one he'd ever seen. She had long straight black hair in a pony-tail and a delicately featured face with slanting almond shaped black eyes, and she was dressed in a blue silk tunic and wide-legged pants. She had a pack on her back and she held a knife in her hand as she crouched ready to attack him again.

Prone on his knees, he watched her, fascinated, as she circled him in a bent-kneed fashion, and gabbled something unintelligible at him.

"I've no the faintest idea what yer saying lassie," he said grinning and rising, she feinted at him with the knife and came at him with a roundhouse kick that was so swift it sent him sprawling on his back. She leapt onto his chest, holding the knife to his throat and gabbled at him some more.

No longer amused, he put up a hand and grabbed her thin wrist, really there was nothing of her, and twisted until the knife fell from her grasp with a cry. Levering himself over, he squashed her flat beneath him on the grass and gripping both her hands he said, "That's enough!"

She wriggled beneath him, and he discovered that she was definitely female, or at least his body thought so. It has been so long since he'd felt anything resembling desire it took him aback. Rising to his feet abruptly, he dragged her up and threw her, pack and all over his shoulder. She shrieked at this treatment and kicked and wriggled and belted him with her fists, but he held her tightly and the dogs came running, barking and capering around him, leaping up and generally making a ruckus.

"Heel!" he snapped at them, and they settled, following him back to the house. This female was one of the accursed Chinese he'd heard so much about. There seemed to be a plague of them suddenly in this corner of the world, all to do, he suspected with his brother. Since he couldn't understand this one, and she seemed somewhat dangerous, it would seem to be prudent to lock her up until he could ascertain what she wanted.

Coming Late 2024

AFTERWORD

The 8 Trigrams rebellion of 1813 was a real event, put down by the Qing Government. But Master Zhanghu-Zi is fictitious. The Neidan Text known as the Golden Elixir does exist in some form as a sacred text of Taoism. And it does speak (in very veiled terms) of a way to seek eternal life through meditation and the raising of the spirit to levels of enlightenment beyond the limitations of the physical.

It is my understanding from my readings that devotees of the religion of the White Lotus do embrace a form of ritual suicide to escape shame or other consequences. If I have misinterpreted this in anyway that is offensive, that was not my intention.

Merlow's use of more advanced medical techniques is based on what I have been able to glean of knowledge possessed by the Ancient Chinese, who certainly understood a great deal more about how to treat and heal the sick effectively, than practitioners of Western medicine at the time this book is set.

Typhus was a disease spread by insect bites and was not transmissible through human contact, although this was not well understood by Western practitioners at this time.

ACKNOWLEDGMENTS

I would like to thank my beta reader Kesha, for her insight and comments on an earlier draft of the book, they were most helpful. In addition I would like to thank Kathy Golden for some last minute insights that were invaluable in improving and strengthening the book.

* * *

Merlow and Hetty were first introduced in Saving Mr Rooke, Seb and Bethany's romance. Turn the page to read an excerpt from their love story.

WREN ST CLAIRE

SAVING Mr ROOKE

VILLAIN'S REDEMPTION BOOK 3.5

ABOUT SAVING MR ROOKE

He rescues kittens and damsels in distress, now she must save him...from his dark past...

When her stepfather tries to force Bethany Whittaker to marry his business partner, Beth does the bravest and most foolish thing she has ever done in her life: she runs away. Unfortunately, her grand plan to catch the stagecoach to Bath, comes a cropper at the first hurdle and she finds herself at the mercy of the worst London at night has to offer a defenceless young woman alone.

Fortunately for her, Mr Sebastian Rooke has been instructed by his employer to find and protect her. Rescuing Beth from the consequences of her own folly is a simple matter for Mr Rooke, getting the enchanting and innocent young woman out of his mind and heart is not.

Saving Mr Rooke is the enchanting extra instalment in the Villain's Redemption Steamy Regency Romance series. This one is like a warm hug but with all the spice! If you like sweet but determined damsel in distress and big, over-protective, soft-hearted heroes and a generous dollop of passionate romance then you'll love Wren St Claire's Sweet and Steamy Regency Romance.

What readers are saying about Saving Mr Rooke:
WOW! Beautifully written, passionate and highly romantic. 10* please!

Reviewed in the United Kingdom on November 6, 2023

Verified Purchase

"Astoundingly sensual. The chemistry and achingly electrifying attraction make this a fantastic read. I'd go so far as saying this is one hell of a turn on - the kind of romantic desire and reverence every woman yearns for. LOVED THIS. "

This novella is a companion volume to **Revenge on the Devil** book 3 of the series and takes place within the timeframe of book 3.

SAVING MR ROOKE

Chapter 1

Recovering debts, extorting information, re-possessing property... Sebastian Rooke passed his week under review looking for a suitable topic for his regular letter to his sister. He sighed and dipped his pen in the ink pot again. It had been a particularly unpleasant week.

A rustle behind him made him turn to see two of the five kittens he had rescued three days ago playing with a piece of bark that had fallen off one of the logs in the fireplace. The hot summer weather that had plagued them for the past month and half had taken a cold turn today, necessitating the lighting of a fire.

Little paws batted at the fragment, making it dance, and two black and white balls of fluff pounced. The pair rolling over and wrestling with each other, the wood was soon forgotten. He smiled at their antics and turned back to his desk. *Kittens! Now that was something he could tell Hetty about. With some judicious editing of course.*

No mention of the circumstances in which he found the kittens. Under the floorboards in a derelict house, that formerly belonged to a rival of his employer, Mr Lovell. That rival was now dead of course. Had been for some time, hence the derelict nature of the house. Mr Rooke and his crew had been occupied in looking for any caches of information or valuables that might have been left behind. They found more than they bargained for, including two rotting corpses, identity unknown and never likely to be as there wasn't enough left of them to identify anything but their gender.

There was no sign of the kitten's mother, and the little things were bleating fit to bring the roof down, which was how Seb discovered them.

Standing in the middle of the wrecked room, sweaty and disheveled, listening to the racket, he bent and ripped up the remaining floorboards with his big, strong hands, until they were revealed, nestled into a rotten blanket. Five sets of enormous eyes stared up at him and five little pink mouths opened in supplication.

His compatriots were all for leaving them or drowning them, but Seb couldn't do that.

So, he found a rat chewed creel and brought them home to his single room apartment in St Giles and fed them milk till they nearly burst. He'd found a shallow wooden box and filled it with earth from the small garden plot that ran along the back and side of his long narrow apartment and set it down near the side door for their toilet.

Twenty minutes later, the letter finished, Seb

reviewed his sisters last letter to ensure he had responded to all her queries. *Except one.* He had no prospects of meeting a respectable woman in his current circumstances and even if he did, his line of work prohibited him taking a wife, so there was no point in responding to *that* question. *Even if he was worthy of a woman who was fit to meet his sister and father...*

Dismissing his lack of marriage prospects with a slight shake of his head and an internal wince, he folded the sheet carefully and put it in an envelope. He addressed it to Miss H Rooke care of the Rectory at Pinner in the Borough of Harrow, and put the envelope on the mantelpiece, careful not to step on the kittens whom, their fight forgotten, had fallen asleep on the hearth rug. The envelop dislodged a shiny brass button, which fell with a clunk to the floor.

Bending slowly to pick it up, Seb cradled it in his palm. At one point that brass button was all he had left of his sanity. It belonged to his soldier's uniform and holding it in his hand was the only thing that brought him back from the madness. The retreat from Salamanca to Corunna had broken the British, the conditions were horrendous and discipline sadly lacking. But it was the slaughter of the horses on top of the horrors of the battle at Corunna that brought him unstuck. Over 4000 horses slain, 900 men lost and 5000 wounded or gravely ill with fever, himself among them.

He had come home a broken man. Numb from the horrors he had witnessed, once his body had recovered, he needed work so as not to be a burden to his family. He became a croupier for Garmon

Lovell and the separation between his feelings and his actions enabled him to do things other men would balk at.

Over the years the numbness persisted, but little things got though his armor occasionally, like little balls of fluff. He smiled at the kittens sleeping by his big booted feet and put the button back on the mantlepiece.

His stomach rumbled, not an unusual occurrence, he was a big man, and it had been several hours since he last ate. He went to the pantry cupboard in the corner of the room and fetched out a generous slice of pork pie and a bottle of porter. He set his meal on the small side table, situated beside the armchair drawn up to the fireplace and lit a candle to supplement the dying summer sunlight coming through the window. Sitting down, he picked up his book.

With the pork pie in his other hand, he took a bite and settled in for a quiet read. It wasn't often he got a night off; the prospect of time alone was pleasant.

Needles in the side of his thigh, made him look down to find another kitten in the act of transferring from the chair up which she had climbed, to his leg, hoisting herself up by her paws, little claws digging in for purchase. This one was tabby with white splotches. He smiled and held out a fragment of meat to the little thing. She took it eagerly, and like magic her brothers and sisters appeared, all clamoring for their share of the treat with little bleating mews.

Breaking off some of the pie and crumbling it into fragments, he set the plate down on the floor and the kittens gathered round it. Rising he fetched a small bowl and filled it with milk. The kittens transferred their attention to the milk, except for one of the boys who seemed more interested in the meat.

"Sensible fellow," murmured Seb approvingly, returning to his seat and his book.

It was several hours later that a loud rapping on his door jerked Seb out of the doze he had fallen into.

"Mr Rooke! Mr Rooke!" an urgent voice called through the letter slot.

It was dark and somewhat chilly, the candle having guttered out and the fire reduced to a few hot coals, the sound of pounding rain lashing the windows, told of a storm of no small proportions.

Rising and creating an avalanche of kittens that had chosen to fall asleep on him, Seb moved groggily towards the door, a hand running through his short dark hair and scratching his stubbled chin. *What the hell's time was it?*

"Aye what's to do?" he rumbled opening the door and finding a drenched and panting young Ben, Mr Lovell's chief mudlark and personal courier, on the doorstep.

"It's Mrs Tate's sister, Miss Whittaker! She's gone missing. We're to find her swift like, Mr Lovell's orders!"

Chapter 2
Some hours earlier

Miss Bethany Whittaker, balanced precariously on the outside of the balcony to her bedroom and gripped the sheet she had tied to the railing with one hand, willing herself to let go of the balustrade with the other. This was the bravest and most foolish thing she had ever done, without a doubt, and fear held her immobile and shaking for a moment that felt like an eternity.

Everything sane in her screamed to clamber back over the balcony rail to safety, but the prospect of what awaited her on the other side if she did, finally goaded her into letting go of the rail and grabbing the sheet with both hands.

Letting herself down, hand over hand on the sheet, had seemed a simple matter when she planned it in her head, but the reality proved otherwise. The ground seemed a long way down and her arms and hands she discovered were not strong enough to hold her weight for any appreciable time. Her muscles taught and shaking, shrieking with the strain, she lowered herself to the end of the sheet and dropped to the grass below, landing in an undignified heap beside her valise, which she had dropped over the balcony earlier.

The summer sun was hovering at the horizon and darkness threatened. It had been hot for weeks, but today the weather had turned sullen, and the clouds were gathering, there was a distinct chill in the air.

After a few moments to catch her breath and still the shaking of her limbs, she rose, pulled the hood of her cloak over her honey-coloured curls and picked up the valise. Straightening her shoulders, she marched towards the back gate of the property's rear garden and let herself out into the alley. *She was not going to marry Josiah Neeps, no matter what her stepfather said, and great Aunt Maddie would ensure it, if only she could get to her.*

Her initial reaction when papa told her that Josiah Neeps had offered for her, was shock. Followed closely by disbelief when it became clear that this proposal had papa's blessing.

"Your sister's unconscionable behaviour makes it imperative you marry swiftly before she ruins all your chances Beth," he said with a regretful smile.

"But Papa-"

"Neeps is a good match. He has a secure job and lives close by, so you won't be far from us. And an older man will treat you kindly Beth."

"Older - he's forty-five!" gasped Beth, putting a hand to her chest where her heart was pounding.

"Beth in your circumstances is it likely that another man will have you?"

"Hiram!" protested her mother feebly.

Hot tears stung her lids, and she sat down hard on the settee behind her. "Papa, I did not plan to marry, you know that!"

"But my dear if something were to happen to me or your mother you would be alone-"

"I would not, Mary and Genevra would look after me!"

"It would not be fair to burden Mary with your care, she has her own family to think of and as for Genevra - she cannot care for herself, let alone you. A widow on her own in that Tavern it's a disgrace!"

"Papa, I do not wish to marry Mr Neeps!" she said earnestly.

"I am your father; you need to trust me that I know what is best for you Bethany."

"No!" she shook her head vehemently. "No! I won't! I will not!"

"Beth -" her mother moved towards her concern in her eyes. "You're distressing yourself, that isn't good for you."

Beth gulped and gasped for breath, rising she clenched her fists. "You can't make me marry him! I won't!"

"Beth I am your father, and you will do as I tell you!" Her stepfather's face turned red, and he raised his fist for emphasis. Not to hit her, he would never do that. All the same, his anger made her flinch. She hated arguments. Papa and Genevra were always fighting, she hated it, so did mama.

She wiped her face and sniffed. "I cannot, papa, I don't love him. I don't even like him! He's creepy and repulsive!"

"Now you're being silly my girl. You have taken some ridiculous notion into you head-" he stopped as if struck by a thought and softened his tone. "It is your female situation that makes you so hysterical. I make every allowance for that. You just need to rest; you will see things more clearly when you are recovered." He turned to mama. "Miriam see that she rests in her room until she is better."

"Papa I'm not ill-"

"I never said you were my dear. I understand these female things can addle the brain. You will be better directly, I am sure. You just need rest. Go to your room."

"Papa-"

"Go to your room Bethany or I will be forced to

carry you there and make you stay!" His colour rose alarmingly again.

"Papa-!"

"Right-" he grabbed her arm and marched her out of the parlour and up the stairs. His grip was tight but not bruisingly so.

"Hiram!" Mama trailed them.

Opening her bedroom, he pushed her through the door gently, and shut it firmly. Beth heard the key turn in the lock.

"You will stay there until you come to your senses!" His implacable voice came through the door. Beth slumped against it, tears sheeting down her cheeks.

"Mama! Mama! Don't let him do this!"

She heard her mother's voice fading as she moved away. "Hiram! Hiram!"

Half an hour after climbing over the balcony, Beth entered the courtyard of the George and Blue Boar Coaching Inn with some trepidation. The journey on foot to this hostelry had all her senses on high alert. Every person she passed seemed a potential threat and her nerves were raw already. She was not, she reflected miserably, cut out for this sort of thing. Her sister Genevra would not turn a hair in like circumstances, but then Genevra was the bravest and most competent person she knew.

Thoughts of Genevra stiffened her backbone. She would have gone to her rather than Aunt Maddie, but she knew their stepfather would just drag her back home from Genevra's, it was too close. He had made no secret of his opinion of

Genevra's ability to look after herself let alone anyone else, he would never let her stay with Genevra.

And his point about her being a burden to Mary had cut her to the quick. Besides Mary was by far too sweet to resist Papa, she would never stand up to him as Genevra did. If she could reach Aunt Maddie in Bath, it was too far away for him to reach her without a lot of botheration, and she suspected he wouldn't go to the effort. She *hoped* he wouldn't.

She looked around the courtyard, lit by lamps hung on poles, it was busy with men, horses and carriages, none of which appeared to be the stage-coach. *Was she at the wrong Inn? No, she was sure this was the inn the stage left from, but at what time?* She approached the entrance, ignoring the stares of the men and their lewd comments, though they made her blush and cringe.

The men at the brewery didn't treat her that way. Having grown up in a brewer's yard she had thought she was at home around men. They were a bit rough round the edges but always treated her politely and with respect. Like Joe, and his boys who had gone to work for Genevra as her tapster when Jacob died. Occasionally she caught snatches of bawdy talk, but they always stopped when they saw her, which was a bit frustrating really. She would like to have heard more.

Inside the entrance, she approached the desk where a man in a buckskin waistcoat sat reading a paper. He didn't look up. She fiddled with her valise and then cleared her throat. Finally, when these elicited no response, she said a little acerbically, "Could you tell me when the stagecoach for Bath is due?"

"You missed it love," he said turning a page of the large broadsheet.

"Oh!" Daunted she said. "When is the next one due?"

"Four o'clock tomorrow, like it always is." He looked up then as her knees went weak with disappointment.

What was she going to do until four o'clock tomorrow? This was not going to plan at all! They would notice she was missing long before that and start looking for her.

"Do you want to buy a ticket?" he asked, looking her up and down as if assessing if she could afford the fare.

She lifted her chin and nodded. *If she bought the ticket she was committed.*

"That'll be one pound twenty-five pence love," he said reaching under the counter for a ticket book.

"One pound twenty-"

"Yes, and you need to tip the driver and the guard so mind you have enough for that as well as a meal while you're on the road. It will take you forty-eight hours to get to Bath, if the roads are clear." He stopped as a loud crack of thunder sounded followed by the splash of sudden rain pounding on the pavement. "Which by the sound of it they won't be." He added.

She swallowed and dug in her purse for the money. She had two pounds and a few pence in her reticule. It had seemed sufficient funds for her journey when she came up with this mad scheme in the safety of her bedchamber. Faced with the realities of daily expenses she realized she may have underestimated the costs involved. Handing over the requisite amount she took the ticket proffered and stuffed it in her reticule.

"How much to stay here for the night?" she asked.

"One pound two shillings including breakfast," he said.

She swallowed again, fighting back the tears that sprang to her eyes. "That is too expensive. Do you have anything cheaper?"

He ran his eyes over her in a way that made her feel uncomfortable. "That depends."

"On what?" she asked, her heart thudding.

He came round the counter and approached her. Standing close to her, he bent and whispered in her ear, "If you choose to warm my bed for the night you can stay free."

She stiffened in horror and recoiled. "No!" She stared at him and as he reached to grab her arm, she turned and bolted out the door through the courtyard and into the street.

The rain was coming down in sheets and had doused the streetlamps, so everything was dark and wet. Sobbing with shock, she ran along the street, heedless of her direction, only wanting to get away from the George and Blue Boar as quickly as she could. The pavement was uneven and the drains awash with water. Her boots and skirts were sodden in moments, and her valise banged against her legs as she ran.

A stitch in her side brought her to a standstill, whimpering with pain and gasping for breath. Her heartbeat wildly out of rhythm, and for a moment of panic she feared she would expire on the spot, that weak organ giving out as she had been repeatedly warned it would.

She had come to a halt near the entrance to another Inn, the Red Lion. Its mullioned widows glowed with a welcoming light, and she stumbled towards the entrance and entered the building to be engulfed in a warm fug of malt and hops. To the daughter of a brewer, such smells were commonplace and comforting. With them came the sounds of convivial conversation and the smell of roasting meat, which made her mouth water. It had been an age since dinner.

The Inn was lined with dark wood and the tapster stood behind the counter serving pots of porter. She approached the counter and waited for the tapster to notice her. Eventually he moved in her direction and asked what he could do for her.

"Do you have a room available for the night?" She tried to keep the tremor out of her voice.

"Aye but you'll have to share."

"With- with a lady?" she asked.

He shook his head.

She backed away and said hastily. "Thank you, no!" and bolted out into the street again. She tried three more hostelries with similar results. Either the tariff was too high, or she had to share, and it seemed there were no single ladies staying in any of the Inns she ventured into.

The rain was still torrential, and she was soaked to the skin when she was assailed by the most heavenly scent of pie emanating from the doorway of yet another Inn. This one was called the Dagger.

Drawn forward on the smell, she caught the door before it could close and ventured within.

Behind the counter was a red cheeked woman of generous proportions conversing with several men to whom she was dispensing pots of porter. Relief at the sight of a woman, gave her strength and she approached her with a tremulous smile.

Spying her, the woman smiled and leaned over the counter. "Good evenin' dearie what can I get ye?"

Beth nodded at the pies lined up on the counter on cooling racks. "Could I have one of you pies please? They smell heavenly."

"O course you can, dearie. Best pies in Lunnon we 'ave. That'll be four pence." she held out her hand and Beth handed over the money. The woman slipped it into her pocket and said, "Let me fetch a plate for ye." she turned away and Beth glanced round the Tavern idly. There were several tables scattered round the room at which men sat enjoying their porters and a meal. She was about to turn back to the counter when her eyes snagged on a familiar balding head.

Cold horror trickled down her spine. *It couldn't be! But it was.* Josiah Neeps chose just that moment to look up from his plate and stare straight at her. She had pushed her hood back from her face, so there was nowhere to hide. She knew the moment he recognised her.

He rose from his seat just as she let out a squeak of horror, and picking up her valise, she bolted out the door into the rain. She glanced back over her shoulder to the sight of Neeps silhouetted in the doorway. He hesitated as if thinking twice about venturing out into the weather, but then seeing her he stepped out, giving chase.

Beth turned and ran, clutching the valise to her chest and fleeing down the street. Crossing to the other side, she darted down a side street and kept running. Turning a corner, she looked back and saw him closing on her. With a whimper of terror, she ran into the alley, almost tripping over her sodden skirts.

She dodged into another, even narrower alley, and came to a halt because it was so dark, she couldn't see a thing. She leaned against the wall panting and trying to listen for pursuit over the thudding in her ears, her gasping breath and the drumming of rain on the pavement and rooves. She waited for what seemed like an eternity until her limbs were so stiff with cold and terror, she had difficulty moving.

Venturing out of the dark alley, she looked for any sign of Neeps and found none. He must have given up. Relief made her knees sag, and she leaned against the wall while tears ran down her cheeks.

Swallowing she straightened and continued down the street looking for somewhere, anywhere to get out of the relentless rain.

Finally, she spied a porch that seemed to offer some shelter. It was somewhat malodorous, but she was past caring. Venturing into it, she leaned against the wall and slowly sank down until she was sitting with her legs drawn up and the wall at her back. She was exhausted and soaked through.

She closed her eyes, telling herself she would just rest awhile and then resume her search for somewhere to stay. With her hand resting on her valise, fatigue overcame her discomfort and she slipped into a fitful doze.

She woke with a start as the valise slipped from under her hand. A skinny urchin, tugged at the valise. Grabbing the valise with a squeak of indignation, Beth tugged back.

"That is mine!" she scolded, batting at the child, who spat at her and uttered a string of obscenities.

"Get off!" Beth pushed to her feet and kicked out at the thief. The child scrabbled at her gown and Beth heard the fabric tear. Getting a better grip on the valise she swung it at the child and the skinny creature backed off and ran.

Horrified at her own behaviour, Beth sank back sobbing. The rain appeared to have eased a bit, so she rose and clutching the valise to her chest, she tried to retrace her steps to find her way back to High Holborn.

Saving Mr Rooke

Want your next FREE book? Turn the page…

Duke
in
Disguise

A Cinderella Romance

Wren St Claire

DUKE IN DISGUISE - FREE BOOK!

Duke in Disguise: A Cinderella Romance A Steamy Georgian Fairy Tale Romance

A feckless hero, a cinderella heroine and an HEA. Romantic and 3 Flames Steamy!

Miss Jocelyn Eden, is an unpaid drudge in the house of her Uncle a strict Methodist. When she is separated from her family during an evangelical mission to the gin-swilling prostitutes of St Giles, London, she is rescued by a handsome, charming and very drunk stranger, dressed only in torn shirt and stained breeches.

Her mysterious rescuer is Costin Layne, a Duke in disguise and refugee from his mother's plot to marry him to a woman he detests.

As these two embark upon a clandestine relationship and fall hopelessly in love, the machinations of their respective families threaten to tear them apart.

But Costin will go to any lengths to give Jocelyn the happily-ever-after she deserves, complete with ball gown and ~~Prince~~ Duke, no matter the price he has to pay.

WANT A COPY OF DUKE IN DISGUISE - FREE?

Go to Wren St Claire to sign up for my newsletter and get your FREE copy of **Duke in Disguise** and lots more goodies.

ABOUT THE AUTHOR

Email me at author@wrenstclaire.com

You can find me hanging out (under my real name) in the HR Facebook groups Ton & the Tartans and Upturned Petticoats and Undone Cravats.

Follow me on Facebook, Bookbub or visit my Website to find out what I'm working on next, or my Amazon Author page to find all my books.

ALSO BY WREN ST CLAIRE

Book 1 in he Villain's Redemption Series
The Devil's Mistress

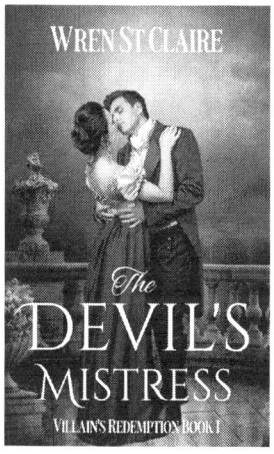

She is his brother's fiancé. Forbidden.

Viviana Torrington longs to be understood.

The toast of the Ton, spoiled beauty, Viviana, wants a man who will see past her wicked nature to the vital, passionate woman beneath, and love her with all her faults. At the end of a stellar season, Viviana accepts the proposal of her most eligible of suitors, but realises her mistake when she meets his irresistibly attractive, charismatic and commanding younger brother, Captain Jack Elliot.

He wasn't looking for love, until he met her.

More than her stunning beauty, Jack saw her vital, shining spirit and knew he'd met his fate. But she is engaged to his brother who loves her, the last thing Jack is willing to do is break his brother's heart.

There is only one recourse open to a man of honour. Leave.

But when Viviana tries to follow Jack, she is kidnapped by another suitor, who wants her and her dazzling fortune, for himself.

How many hearts can one woman break, in her search for redemption and love?

The Devil's Mistress is the delightful first book in the Villain's Redemption, Steamy Regency Romance series. If you like flawed heroines, sizzling tension and irresistible heroes, then you'll love Wren St Claire's passionate romance.

What Readers are saying:

"Wren St Claire's writing brings Kerrigan Byrne, Elisa Braden and Elizabeth Hoyt to mind. Her stories are so rich and she has a great way of making the reader root for morally grey characters." Reader's comment

Masterful, moody and magnificent!

Reviewed in the United Kingdom on November 4, 2023

<u>Verified Purchase</u>

★★★★★

"Beautifully written, passionate and totally captivating. Haven't read a historical romance for ages but loved this - now onto book 2! HIGHLY RECOMMENDED. "

Book 2 in the Villain's Redemption Series

Taming the Devil

She destroyed all his plans with one shot from her pistol...now he will turn the world upside down to have her.

Miss Diana Lovell is a woman thirsting for revenge. She blames the late Duke of Mowbray for her father's demise and ruining her life. She reasons that the current Duke is cut from the same cloth as his grandsire and she means to get what is hers by right, no matter the cost. But she doesn't bargain on the magnetic attraction that sparks between her and the current Duke and finds herself drawn into an intimate and dangerous proximity with a man she cannot resist or get away from.

Sir Anthony "Devil" Harcourt is now the 7th Duke of Mowbray, but with the title comes a mountain of debt and a reckoning, as the sins of his grandfather come crashing down upon him in the form of a beautiful virago bent on revenge and obtaining what is hers. Anthony's cold heart is not easily softened, yet the moment he sets eyes on Diana he knows he will never let her go. The trouble is the lady has other ideas.

Passion explodes when these two souls collide and bitter, cynical Anthony discovers that love may be possible after all, if he can only redeem himself sufficiently to deserve it.

Taming the Devil is the sizzling HOT second book in the Villain's Redemption, Steamy Regency Romance series. If you like wicked heroes with a dark past, spicy, passionate romance and feisty heroines, then you'll love Wren St Claire's deliciously wicked romance.

Book 3 in the Villain's Redemption Series

Revenge on the Devil

A man with no heart.

Until he meets her.

A stubborn independent widow, in need of his protection, ironically from himself.

Seven nights of passion. Will either of them survive with their hearts intact?

Garmon Lovell has never allowed himself to love anyone. Until he meets her.

A man hardened by his past and obsessed with exacting revenge on those who have wronged him. When his men mistakenly capture Genevra Tate, a determined woman desperate to hang onto her late husband's Tavern, Garmon finds himself irresistibly drawn to her strength as much as her luminous beauty.

A passion like she has never known...but it will take more than passion to mend Genevra's shattered heart.

Genevra swears she will never trust a man again. To buy a stay of execution on her husband's gambling debt, Genevra offers the only currency she has: a night in Garmon's bed.

The sparks that fly between them could set London on fire.

As the hard man falls hard, Garmon's tender care for her, threatens Genevra's vulnerable heart. Yet when disaster strikes, is there anywhere else to turn, but to the man who swears he will kill and die for her?

Revenge on the Devil is the searingly passionate 3rd book in the Villain's Redemption Steamy Regency Romance series. If you like strong but soft-centred heroes, steamy passion, tender and touching romance with all the feels, then you'll love Wren St Claire's heart-rending Steamy Regency Romance.

10* please! This is awesome!❤

Reviewed in the United Kingdom on November 6, 2023
<u>Verified Purchase</u>

"If you want a hot steamy romance with plenty of deadly excitement (and who doesnt?!) then this is for you. I went through every emotion reading this and was reminded of one of Grimms dark fairytales! Please give this book a try and once you've done so read the whole series cos they're all brill!!! 💕 🔥 🖤 💞 "

"Hot and tender, this book will melt your heart – and your kindle!" readers comment.

"This was such an amazing story! It's rare to find such a good book with the ability to move me to tears, has the steam and makes me happy all in the same book." - readers comment

Book 3.5 in the Villain's Redemption Series

Saving Mr Rooke: A Sweet and Steamy Age-Gap Novella

He rescues kittens and damsels in distress, now she must save him...from his dark past...

When her stepfather tries to force Bethany Whittaker to marry his business partner, Beth does the bravest and most foolish thing she has ever done in her life: she runs away. Unfortunately, her grand plan to catch the stagecoach to Bath, comes a cropper at the first hurdle and she finds herself at the mercy of the worst London at night has to offer a defenceless young woman alone.

Fortunately for her, Mr Sebastian Rooke has been instructed by his employer to find and protect her. Rescuing Beth from the consequences of her own folly is a simple matter for Mr Rooke, getting the enchanting and innocent young woman out of his mind and heart is not.

Saving Mr Rooke is the enchanting extra instalment in the Villain's Redemption Steamy Regency Romance series. This one is like a warm hug but with all the spice! If you like sweet but determined damsel in distress and big, over-protective, soft-hearted heroes and a generous dollop of passionate romance then you'll love Wren St Claire's Sweet and Steamy Regency Romance.

5.0 out of 5 stars

WOW! Beautifully written, passionate and highly romantic. 10* please! 💘

Reviewed in the United Kingdom on November 6, 2023

Verified Purchase

Astoundingly sensual. The chemistry and achingly electrifying attraction make this a fantastic read. I'd go so far as saying this is one hell of a turn on - the kind of romantic desire and reverence every woman yearns for. LOVED THIS. 🔥💘💞❤️💘

Book 4 in the Villain's Redemption Series

Seducing the Sea Devil

An Irish Rogue finds himself press-ganged by a bunch of desperate women.

Heaven or hell?

When Connor Mor leaves Garmon's office that fateful Monday in June 1815, he walks into an ambush set by a bunch of desperate female pirates, bent on pressing men for their crew. When he wakes up on the Sea Devil they are already in the North Atlantic Ocean and there is no way he is getting back to London in a hurry.

Mor gets his comeuppance at the hands of ruthless Pirate Captain Callista Montmayne

Meeting the Sea Devil's Captain, Callista Montmayne, a blonde, blue-eyed, force of nature, dressed in breeches and a battered tricorn hat, he sees an opportunity to seize control of the ship through seducing it's gorgeous captain. He doesn't bargain on Callista's strength and single mindedness.

Callista Montmayne is a woman bent on revenge and nothing and no one is going to distract her, not even a handsome Irishman who thinks he's God's gift to women. But that doesn't mean she can't enjoy what he's got to offer in her bed.

As Callista turns the tables on Connor, they negotiate shipboard politics and the dangers of the sea, to maintain her power base and chase down notorious slaver-captain, Raphael Jose Perez. Callista's obsession with catching Perez is all consuming and leaves no room for love in her damaged heart. Which is a problem for Connor, because he's fallen for the captain, hook, line and sinker.

Seducing the Sea Devil is the final (for now) flaming HOT volume in the Villain's Redemption Steamy Regency Romance series. This one is dark and gritty, action-packed adventure, with all the spice! If you're hankering for a heroine who can hold her own in a man's world, while sheltering her vulnerable heart from pain, you'll love powerful and passionate Callista. If you want a hero secure enough to handle her, you'll adore Connor. And you'll love Wren St Claire's passionate, high-stakes pirate adventure Regency Romance.

So good!

Reviewed in the United States on January 13, 2024

Verified Purchase

"What a totally original story. Brilliant. I absolutely loved Callista and Connor and the whole cast of characters. Each had their own dimension and contributed to the story. The plot was wonderful and unlike any I have read before. Wren St.Claire has a wonderful imagination and is so gifted. She brings intensity, emotion, drama, and love in all of her books. Wonderful!"

"For those who love the swashbuckling adventure of Pirates of the Caribbean and the grittiness of Black Sails but with hot romance..." Reader's comment.

"Wren St Claire's writing brings Kerrigan Byrne, Elisa Braden and Elizabeth Hoyt to mind. Her stories are so rich and she has a great way of making the reader root for morally grey characters." Reader's comment.

Other Regency Romance

The Assassin's Wife

The Missing Heir

Printed in Great Britain
by Amazon

52664069R00159